"Good morning. It's Tuesday, July 2, 1996...."

The television froze Houston in place, her attention riveted to the screen.

Quinn stood up immediately and turned the television off. He stood facing Houston, his body partially hiding the equipment behind him, and said nothing.

"How did you do that?" she asked hoarsely. "It's a tape, right?" Of course. It had to be. How could he record something that hadn't happened yet? "It's some kind of trick," she insisted. "How did you do that?"

And who are you and what are you doing here and why won't you answer me?

Because she didn't want to hear the answers. Quinn knew that, and so did she.

Dear Reader,

You're about to meet another American Romance Heartbeat hero—and this one's definitely "out of this world"!

Undoubtedly, Rebecca Flanders has brought us some memorable men in her past books. But Quinn—the time traveler trapped three hundred years in the past—is sure to provide memories you'll cherish for years to come.

We're delighted by your response to the first several HEARTBEAT titles, and we hope you continue to enjoy this program of American Romance novels featuring unusual plot twists or unmistakably unique heroes!

Sincerely,

Debra Matteucci
Senior Editor & Editorial Coordinator
Harlequin
300 East 42nd Street
New York, NY 10017

Rebecca Flanders

QUINN'S WAY

Harlequin Books

TORONTO • NEW YORK • LONDON
AMSTERDAM • PARIS • SYDNEY • HAMBURG
STOCKHOLM • ATHENS • TOKYO • MILAN
MADRID • WARSAW • BUDAPEST • AUCKLAND

ISBN 0-373-16558-7

QUINN'S WAY

Copyright © 1994 by Donna Ball, Inc.

Chapter One

Until the spaceman fell out of her apple tree, Houston Malloy was having a perfect morning.

For the first time in over a month, she didn't have bus duty, cafeteria duty or a parent-teacher conference. Mark had gotten up with her first call, hadn't complained too much about his breakfast and had even brushed his teeth without being told. Houston had fifteen minutes before she had to leave for school, which allowed her plenty of time for a second cup of coffee and her favorite pastime—taking in the view from her kitchen window.

It was the middle of May, and Iowa farm country had never been more beautiful. Houston liked to get up early, even on school days, just to watch the light spread over the meadow, which on this particular morning was bedecked in spring green, butter cream yellow and morning glory blue. Her neighbor's sheepdog, Arthur, was chasing a honey bee beneath the low-hanging branches of the apple tree—he was not very bright, Arthur—and her calico cat was dozing in a gentle patch of sun on the windowsill. It was precisely the kind of peaceful bucolic scene Houston had moved to the country to enjoy.

She turned away to refill her coffee cup, and when she looked back a humanoid creature in a silver jumpsuit and helmet was tumbling out of the apple tree.

The coffee cup slipped out of her fingers and crashed to the floor, splattering her shoes and the hem of her skirt with coffee before she jumped out of the way. Arthur the sheepdog went into a fit of crazed barking and Heloise the cat shrieked and took off across the lawn in a black-and-orange-and-white blur. Mark clattered down the stairs, shouting, "Hey, Mom, you won't believe what's going on in the meadow!"

But Houston was already running across the front porch, the screen door banging behind her.

By the time she reached him, the alien—or whatever he was—had managed to get to his feet, apparently unharmed, and was now trying to fend off the attentions of an overexcited Arthur, who couldn't decide whether to lick the stranger's face, defend the apple tree from attack or chase the cat. The stranger, for his part, was muttering angrily what must have been curses, while alternately trying to chase the dog away and gather up something that had spilled on the ground.

Houston, when she was within ten feet of him, slowed her approach, regarding him warily. He was without a doubt the strangest thing she had seen in her meadow in quite some time. The formfitting silver jumpsuit displayed every muscle and plane, ripple and bulge, and though a few of those were quite interesting, curiosity was not enough to override caution. His head and face were completely covered by an oval helmet made of some kind of black plastic or glass, completely unlike anything she had ever seen before. In fact, *everything* about him was unlike anything she had ever seen before.

Mark ran up and she grabbed him by the shoulder, watching the scene before her with growing concern. The dog was barking and circling the stranger, and Houston could now see that what he was trying to pick up from the ground were small instruments, like computer tools, and little pieces of black plastic. Apparently something had been broken in the fall.

Abruptly, the man pulled off his helmet, running his hand through a headful of squashed sandy curls, and glared at her. "What are you staring at?" he demanded.

Houston took a startled step backward. "I beg your pardon, but it's not every day a man wearing a silver lamé catsuit falls out of my apple tree. What *are* you doing here?"

"Experiencing a crisis, if you don't mind. Is this your beast?"

He bent down again to search the ground, and Arthur, apparently encouraged by his audience, lunged for him. Mark broke away from Houston and ran to Arthur, grabbing him by the collar while keeping a curious eye on the stranger.

On further study, Houston decided he probably wasn't a spaceman, after all. Curly brown hair and clear hazel eyes seemed to her distinctly all-American traits, and she doubted whether the kind of curses he was muttering were taught on the average alien planet. It was just that bizarre outfit he was wearing ... that and the fact that he appeared out of thin air between one blink of her eye and the next.

Houston looked around. No car, no horse, no motorcycle, not even a bungie cord from which he might have conceivably catapulted out of a hovering helicopter. She took a cautious, protective step toward Mark. "Where in the world did you come from?"

He barely spared her a glance. "Clarion, Minnesota. Excuse me, young man. If you could hold that animal back a little farther I'd be grateful."

Mark voiced one of the questions that was uppermost in Houston's mind. "How did you get here?"

He didn't glance up. "That's a rather complicated story."

Houston looked at her son, thinking out loud. "Sky diver?"

Mark shook his head. He was a studious child, his eyes alert and thoughtful behind Clark Kent-type glasses, and far too serious for a ten-year-old. He could always be counted on to point out the obvious. "No parachute," he replied.

Houston took another look at the man's shiny suit. "Well, eliminating the spaceman theory—"

"Great son of a cat!" the man exclaimed, and Houston threw him a startled look, stepping quickly closer to her son.

The man straightened up with both hands full of tiny machine parts and scraps of grass, his expression disgusted and dismayed. "Look at that! Everything broken, scattered, filled with dirt—" Suddenly his expression changed. Houston thought she could actually see color drain from his face. "Where's my...?" His hand went to his belt line— though he was wearing no belt—as though he expected to find something there. When he didn't, he turned to search the ground again, a new desperation in his movements.

Houston took Mark's shoulders in a unifying gesture—mother, son and sheepdog against the Intruder. "Who are you?" she demanded. "What are you doing here?"

He replied impatiently, "I hardly think any of that matters now—"

"Excuse me!" Exasperation sharpened the challenge in Houston's tone. "Since you're the trespasser here, it seems to me that it should matter a great deal! This is my apple tree and my meadow, and unless you can give me a good reason for not calling the police—"

Arthur apparently decided at that moment that he had been still long enough. With one good lunge, he broke Mark's grip and bounded out of reach. The stranger ducked back against the tree to avoid Arthur's enthusiastic movements, and after one or two wild circles around the group, the sheepdog took off across the meadow in search of more interesting games.

The stranger stood up, dusting off his knees and muttering, "Well, that's just perfect. If anything else can go wrong—"

"You're making a movie!" Houston exclaimed suddenly. "That's it!"

Mark glanced around and reminded his mother, "No crew. A movie crew has lots of equipment, and it would take a couple of eighteen-wheelers to get it all out here. I read somewhere—"

"So he's the advance man," Houston interrupted, a little too anxious to find an explanation. "That's it, isn't it? You're making a movie."

He looked at her, and she knew that wasn't it. He looked at her, and she knew a lot of things about him.... That he had eyes that couldn't lie, a temper he didn't often show and the kind of face a woman wouldn't easily forget. If he had been a teacher, every girl in class would have a crush on him. If he had been a policeman or a fireman, someone would have persuaded him to pose for their annual charity calendar, and he would have been too nice to refuse. If he had been an athlete he would have been the darling of the media, and if he had been a movie star she would have known it.

He could have been any of those things, but he was none of them. Still, there was something about him that made her heart beat a little faster, just looking at him; something above the ordinary, larger than life... something oddly familiar. The set of the mouth, the little scar bisecting the corner of one eyebrow... Where had she seen him before?

He released a soft breath, and she became aware that he was examining her with a scrutiny similar to her own. She felt her cheeks warm, but she wasn't sure whether it was from embarrassment or excitement. What *was* it about this man?

And why in the world couldn't he have found clothing that fitted him more loosely?

"The name is Quinn," he said, with deliberate politeness, "and I am not a spaceman or a sky diver or a movie maker. I'm a field historian on a research project who is, at the moment, just a little lost. My equipment is in a shambles and one very important piece of it is missing—a piece, I might add, that if I don't find I'll be in more trouble than even I want to think about—so please forgive me if I've inconvenienced you but I have far, far bigger problems."

"What's a field historian?" Mark asked.

Houston couldn't stop staring at him. "Have we met?"

For the first time since falling out of the tree, he looked surprised. Those clear hazel eyes moved over her again, toe to head, and lingered on her face. Then he looked away and answered abruptly, "No. I would have remembered."

In that moment Houston almost thought she could put her finger on what it was about him that fascinated her so. But just as she was about to grasp it, a familiar sound distracted her attention and Mark said, "School bus."

She turned toward the road just in time to see the big yellow bus round the curve in front of their house. Mark sometimes rode the bus on Houston's early days, but today they were riding to school together. What the appearance of the bus meant was that she had less than twenty minutes to get to her classroom.

"Perfect," she muttered. So much for her leisurely morning. She turned Mark toward the house and gave him a gentle push. "Okay, run and get your books together. I'm right behind you."

He gave the stranger a last skeptical look, then did as he was instructed.

Houston looked back to Quinn. "Look," she said, "I've got to go to work. Just get out of here, okay? Whatever you're doing, just don't do it here. And..." She had started to leave him but turned back. "If you're planning on burgling the place, please don't break any windows. They're all odd sized and hard to replace."

He had resumed his search of the ground, and he looked up with another spark of surprise. Then he smiled. "Don't worry, I won't."

He had an absolutely incredible smile.

Houston hurried back to the house, knowing she really should call the police and give them a description of the stranger, just in case. But there was something about that face, that smile... Besides, she really didn't have time.

"Don't worry, Mom," Mark assured her as he buckled himself into the front seat of the car beside her. "He's pretty strange, but I don't think he's dangerous. I sure would like to check out his story, though."

Houston looked into the eyes of her wise little man and felt the urge to hug him hard. Mark was at an age where he did not always appreciate such spontaneous gestures of affection, however, so she settled for tousling his hair lightly. "I'm sure you're right, honey. He's probably just some kook who likes to climb trees."

"Probably," agreed Mark. "But I'll keep an eye on him."

Houston's pride was mitigated with concern. She was proud of him because he was so grown up, and she was concerned because he was so grown up. She and Mark's father had divorced when Mark was six, and since then it seemed Mark had grown more and more serious, more and more responsible. She wished sometimes he could just relax and be a kid.

When a ten-year-old child felt he needed to protect his mother from strangers, something was seriously out of balance.

But as it turned out, the entire discussion was moot. As Houston slowed the car at the end of the driveway before turning out onto the road, she deliberately looked back and searched the area around the apple tree. The stranger was gone.

QUINN KNEW that he was in trouble. He was completely lost, the most important things he owned were in pieces that he was not entirely sure he would be able to put together again, and he had no idea how to get back where he belonged.

This would not have ordinarily been a problem of life or death importance, but where Quinn belonged was approximately three hundred years in the future.

The malfunction that had brought him here must have been with the frequency resonator—the same resonator that was now nowhere to be found and without which he had no chance of ever getting home. He tried to recall if there was anything he had done or not done that could have possibly caused this to happen but quickly abandoned the effort. He would leave problems analysis to the button-punchers back home. The only thing he had to worry about now was how to get there.

Quinn was one of the foremost researchers of his time, in many ways a pioneer in his field. That was not a distinction one earned by being unprepared for emergencies. He quickly began to prioritize his needs.

In the storage compartment of his helmet he had money, some undamaged tools and a few essential micronics that would enable him to interface with the computers of this time. Beneath his protective suit he wore a costume appropriate—more or less—to this decade. Matters could have been worse.

The first priority on this, as any other mission, was to establish a cover and a base of operations. Food, shelter, the elements of survival were necessities that could not be pushed aside by any other concern. So the first order of business was to find out where and *when* he was, so that he could establish an identity in this time and set up a base.

The search for the frequency resonator was paramount, but he had to be prepared for the fact that it might have been lost during transfer and might never be found. He would have to begin work immediately on repairing the tracking device, using the equipment he had with him and the materials of this century that would enable him to find the resonator if it was in this time period.

But in the meantime, there was his mission and no excuse for abandoning it. Even if he could not return home, there was always the chance that the information he gathered could.

One thing was certain. He was attracting far too much attention here, in the middle of nowhere rec-

ognizable, dressed as he was. The way the woman
had looked at him... The way the woman had looked
at him made his pulse beat faster even now, remem-
bering her.

Some of the surprises on this trip were not entirely unpleasant. Maybe she was a sign of better
things to come.

He watched her walk back toward the house, then
looked around for a place in which to change into his
"civilian" clothes. There was a closed garage and a
couple of outbuildings close to the house, but given
what she had said about burglars, it was probably
wiser not to give her any more cause for suspicion—
particularly since he was going to need her permission if he was to continue to search her property for
the resonator.

Memorizing his landmarks, he checked the contents of the storage area in his helmet one more time.
He took out a small metal holder and opened it,
looking at the contents soberly for a moment.
Twenty-three small tablets were contained inside the
case, one for each day he was expected to be here.
When the pills ran out, so would his time.

It was not a comforting thought.

But Quinn was an explorer by trade, an adventurer by nature, and he was not easily daunted. He
had been in tight spots before and had always found
his way out; he would no doubt do so again. Here he
was in the twentieth century, that mad and reckless
time where anything was possible and every breath

was an adventure; if he had to be stranded, he could think of no place better to be.

He would find his way home. He always did.

Swinging his helmet by its strap over his shoulder, he set off down the road, feeling like a trailblazer discovering the promised land—which, in his own way, he was.

HOUSTON TAUGHT third grade at Carsonville Elementary School, which was enough of a challenge to put all thoughts of everything else out of her mind even on an ordinary day. With twenty-eight active eight-year-olds all suffering from spring fever, this was by no means an ordinary day. There were two fights, one lost lunch box and one playground accident. The class gerbil escaped. After eight-thirty that day, Houston barely gave the man in the silver suit another thought.

Just when she thought she might get through the day with her sanity intact, she was called to the office for a phone call.

The sheepish voice on the other end made her stomach clench.

"Hi, hon. Look, I'm sorry for bothering you at school..."

"I have asked you not to call me here, Mike," Houston reminded her ex-husband as politely as she could manage. She was acutely aware of the school secretary a few feet away, who was trying a little too hard to pretend she wasn't listening. "It's hard for me to get away from the classroom."

"I know, and I really hate to do it, but I've got a little emergency here." He gave one of those phony, self-deprecating laughs that set her teeth on edge. "Yeah, I know it's not the first time."

"What's the problem?" Houston inquired tightly. She knew what the problem was, and she didn't particularly want to hear it. But she also knew hearing it was inevitable.

"Nothing seventy-five dollars couldn't fix."

Houston didn't know whether to be relieved or infuriated. It could have been triple that amount, so she was relieved. But seventy-five dollars was seventy-five she couldn't spare, and she was furious.

She deliberately turned her back on the secretary—and found herself looking straight into the face of her principal, Millie Shores. Millie was more than Houston's principal, she was also her best friend. She stood now leaning against the doorway of her office with a very disapproving look on her face. Millie was of the opinion that ex-husbands, like old horses, should be humanely put to sleep when they had outlived their usefulness.

Houston said to Mike, "I thought you had gotten that job over in Sable." She didn't want to be having this conversation over the phone; she knew it was a battle she couldn't win and she didn't know why she even wasted the energy trying. Habit, perhaps.

"I did," he insisted. "But that's the thing—first check isn't for two weeks and I've got to have gas money, don't I? I'll pay you back, hon, first check."

"Now where have I heard that before?" Houston murmured. She knew it was futile, but she just couldn't resist.

He bristled—or pretended to. "Hey, do you think I like this? Do you think I like being unemployed, begging my ex-wife for grocery money?"

"As a matter of fact," Houston said, "I do."

The hurt silence on the other end of the phone was astonishingly convincing. Houston felt remorse creeping through her like some insidious parasite, turning her spine to jelly.

His tone was subdued as he said, "I'm sorry I bothered you."

"No, wait." Houston couldn't believe those words were coming out of her mouth. She hated herself.

She sighed, and her own tone dropped a fraction as she said, "I know you're trying. All right. But, Mike, you can't keep doing this."

"Great." He cheered immediately. "Just drop it in the mail, will you? To my mother's address. Thanks, hon!"

The final bell of the day rang as she hung up the phone, feeling like the world's biggest chump.

Millie beckoned her into her office, her expression stern. "You," she informed her, "are a professional doormat."

Houston groaned. "I know."

"If you stood up to the kids in your class the way you stand up to that leech you call an ex-husband, the animals would be running the zoo."

Houston sank into the chair beside the door, sighing as she tugged loose the band that held her mass of bright red curls into an unruly semblance of a ponytail. "I know."

"The guy owes you over ten thousand dollars in back child support and you're giving *him* money!"

"I know, I know. I'm a wimp and a sucker and if there were a law against stupidity I'd be doing ten to life." She rebundled the ponytail into a slightly neater mass and stuffed it back into the elastic band.

"Why do you let him do this to you?"

"Because it's easier to pay him than to listen to him whine."

Millie leaned against the desk, folded her arms across her chest and looked as though she was going to launch into an extremely familiar lecture. Houston met her stare for stare, however, and in the end all she said was, "Other than that, how's life treating you?"

Houston considered the question as she pushed up the sleeves of her sweater, noticed a spaghetti-sauce stain on her cuff and tried to brush off a smear of plaster of paris that seemed to have become embedded in the weave of her skirt.

"The car's acting up again," she said. "I've got another leak in the roof. Kelly Cramer threw up on Jeff Holbrook's new jacket—guess who Jeff's mother is going to blame for *that?* And—oh yeah, a man wearing nothing but a silver jumpsuit fell out of my apple tree this morning.''

Millie lifted an eyebrow. "Good-looking?"

Houston grinned. "You bet."

"There, you see? Things are looking up." Millie turned to start packing her briefcase. "I hope you didn't let him get away. This might have been the one."

Houston shook her head ruefully. "What is it with you happily married women? You can't let anybody be single in peace."

"I'd just like to prove to you that all men aren't like that blight on the face of humanity you married the first time."

"I know that. I don't have to marry the first thing in pants I see to prove it."

Millie closed her briefcase and turned to Houston with a puzzled frown. "What was he doing in your apple tree?"

Houston stood with a shrug. "I don't have a clue. I think he was making a movie."

"In a silver jumpsuit?"

They started down the hall. "A great-*fitting* silver jumpsuit."

They looked at each other and grinned.

They made their way down the hall against the stream of noisy, exuberant children, occasionally halting a crime in progress with a stern look or a sharply called name. That those crimes were nothing more serious than a book in the process of being thrown or a wall about to be defaced with a pencil was only one of the reasons Houston had chosen to bring up her son in a small town and to teach in a rural elementary school.

Millie asked, "Do you want me to send Len over to look at your roof?"

Millie's husband, Len, was the most mechanically incompetent man Houston had ever known. Millie knew that. Len knew that. Nonetheless, Millie felt obliged to volunteer Len to fix whatever went wrong in Houston's life—because, presumably, he was a man and Millie's to volunteer.

"Sure," responded Houston. "He can look at it and tell me what a good job I did fixing it."

They stopped by Houston's classroom to pick up her papers and books, then stepped out into the sun-splashed walkway. Millie grimaced and dug in her purse for sunglasses. "God, I hate this time of year. Why can't we skip right from Christmas to summer vacation?"

Houston chuckled. "You've got to be the only person in the world who hates spring."

"Me and several hundred other elementary school principals. I mean, look at them. These kids are wild."

"Spring fever," Houston agreed.

"You're lucky Mark's such a sweet boy. Good student, too."

"The other kids pick on him."

"They always pick on the smart kids."

"Nerds, you mean."

Millie was indignant. "Mark is not a nerd!"

"I know that," Houston admitted. "It's just that he worries me sometimes. He doesn't have many friends, and he's so serious. He's driving me crazy wanting a CD-rom for his computer. Why can't he want roller blades like the other kids? What is a CD-rom, anyway?"

"About six hundred dollars."

"Great."

"He's probably going to grow up to be another Stephen Hawking."

"Or Ted Bundy."

"Could be. I understand that his mother was a pessimist, too."

Houston spotted Mark across the parking lot, struggling to keep his backpack from slipping off his narrow shoulders. She waved to him. "Well, I'd better get my little genius—or serial killer—home. It looks like he has a lot of homework, and I have to stop by the hardware store for shingles."

Millie stopped walking. "Listen, Houston. This might not be the best time to bring this up, but Karen has spoken to me again about putting Mark up a grade. She'll be calling you, but I thought you'd want to be thinking about it."

Karen was Mark's teacher, and they had had this discussion before. And every time they had it, Houston ended up feeling like a bad mother.

She said reluctantly, "You know how I feel about skipping grades, Millie."

"I wish we had a gifted program here, but we don't. The best we can do is try to keep our exceptional students from becoming bored with their grade-level work. And since he'll be going to middle school next year, anyway, the jump won't be so drastic as it would have been this year."

"But what about social development?"

Millie smiled sympathetically and patted her arm. "You think about it. Talk it over with Mark."

Houston nodded, straightening her shoulders. "Right. Just another one of those average, run-of-the-mill, life-changing decisions to make."

Houston started for her car.

"Do you want to go to Jordo's for dinner?"

Houston grimaced. "Sorry. Can't afford it."

She grinned as Millie threw up her hands in exasperation and walked off.

Chapter Two

There was no accepted scientific theory to back it, but one thing Quinn had discovered in his experience as a time traveler was a certain tendency toward predestination, even synchronicity, in the universe. He had discovered during the course of the day that he was in a place called Carsonville, Iowa, in the United States of America. The date was May 21, 1994, which meant he was only ten years and several hundred miles off target. The population of Carsonville and its surrounding county was 18,621. He was walking along the side of the highway some five miles north of his original landing site in the apple tree of one angry red-haired lady, yet he was not at all surprised to see—of all 18,621 possible candidates—that same angry red-haired lady standing beside the raised hood of a stalled car just ahead.

Synchronicity. Someday he would write a paper.

Her expression grew puzzled as he approached. His traveling clothes were stored at the bottom of the canvas duffel he carried over his shoulder, and he was wearing the chambray shirt and denim pants that seemed to be the uniform of the middle classes for most of the last half of the twentieth century. She didn't recognize him immediately, which was no surprise.

He, on the other hand, could not have mistaken her had she been one of a hundred women in a crush at a New York subway stop, instead of standing alone on the side of an empty rural highway. She was wearing the same print shirtwaist and white canvas shoes she had been wearing that morning, of course, and her wildly curly strawberry-colored hair was drawn away from her face.

The sun was in her eyes, and she squinted to shade them. The wind blew her skirt between her legs and then billowed it away again, shaping and caressing her body. Tiny curls escaped their binding and played around her head like a halo. Sunlight highlighted every freckle on her face and turned her eyes into crinkled pools of cellophane.

Looking at her, Quinn felt his breath catch and his steps slow ever so slightly. In the vastness and glory of this incredible century there were many scenes that were etched indelibly on Quinn's mind, but never had one affected him with its simple unadorned beauty the way the sight of that slender red-haired woman in the windblown dress did.

The picture she made, leaning against the broken car in her yellow print dress with the empty road curving behind her and the wind and the sun playing with the curves of her body was a masterpiece someone had forgotten to paint. It was a portrait he wanted to capture in his mind forever, to hold like a talisman against the barren lonely days that were sure to come.

He was about ten feet from her then, and she must have noticed the odd expression on his face, the slowing of his steps, because her own expression changed as she looked at him more closely. It was then that she recognized him. Surprise and wariness mingled on her face, and she turned to say something to her son, who was studying the network of wire and hoses under the hood of the car as though they formed some words he could read.

Quinn smiled as he grew within speaking distance. "Hi," he said. "Having trouble?"

The boy was looking at him with frank curiosity. The woman was still cautious—and a little disbelieving. "It *is* you, isn't it? The man from the apple tree!"

He grinned and shifted his duffel to the other shoulder, extending his hand. "I'm not sure that's how I want to be known from now on. The name is Quinn."

"Yes, I remember," she murmured uncertainly. Then she seemed to come to a decision and accepted his handshake. "My name is Houston Malloy, and this is my son, Mark."

Her hand was small and strong, and he tried not to hold it too long before turning to nod to Mark. "Nice to meet you both."

But the boy was not so easily impressed. He regarded Quinn skeptically and asked, "What are you doing way out here?"

He answered, "I've been to town."

Houston stared. "On *foot?*"

"It's the best way to see the country."

A moment of silence fell in which he felt himself the object of intense scrutiny by the boy and abject curiosity by the woman, and in which he tried very hard not to be too fascinated by the way the sunlight sparkled in her eyes. He had always found it a good practice not to become too involved with the locals, at least not until he had his cover story well established. With such an inauspicious beginning as he had had with this family, it was more important than ever that he not expose himself to many hard-to-answer questions. On the other hand, his only chance of returning home might well be lying somewhere beneath her apple tree right now. He would have to go back eventually to search, and that search would be a great deal easier with the permission of the property owner.

Synchronicity? Or serendipity?

He nodded toward the car. "Would you like me to take a look?

Houston hesitated, clearly debating the odds against a man who preferred to travel on foot knowing anything at all about repairing an automobile. Then she shrugged. "It won't do any good. It's the timing belt or the alternator or something major like that. It's always something major—and expensive—on this car. Someone we know will be by sooner or later. I'll get a ride home and call the tow truck."

Quinn let his duffel bag slide to the ground, then moved to examine the internal components of the car. Mark watched him closely, and so did Houston.

She knew she should be suspicious. First the man appeared out of nowhere in a place no one had any business being and with no good explanation for his presence there, and then he just happened to be hiking down the highway at the same moment her car broke down. Coincidence? Maybe. Probably. What else, in fact, could it be? But there was something very strange about this man...and perhaps the strangest thing was that it was so easy to trust him.

Quinn turned to take a small pouch of tools from his duffel bag and returned to the engine compartment, muttering something about combustion engines.

Houston moved closer. "What did you say?"

"He said the concept of the internal combustion engine was a mistake," Mark informed her.

Houston muttered, "I can't say I disagree with him there."

She tried to peer over his shoulder as he took one tiny instrument after another from the pouch. "What are those—wrenches?"

He grunted in reply.

"Must be for imports, huh?"

Mark said, "I don't think they're wrenches, Mom."

The instruments spun and hissed, punctuated by Quinn's mutterings under his breath. Mark looked disgusted. "I don't know what you're doing, mister, but it's not going to work."

"Really," Houston said anxiously, "I appreciate your trying to help but it's no problem. This happens all the time." It was beginning to occur to her that what might have been a minor breakdown could easily become an irreparable problem if she allowed this obviously inexperienced stranger to continue to do things beneath the hood. Even Mark disapproved.

Quinn straightened up and tucked the tools back into their pouch. His hands were not even greasy. "Try it now," he said.

Houston regarded him skeptically.

"The engine," he repeated, as though she might have misunderstood him the first time. "Turn it on."

What was it about men that made them so certain that all it took was the magical touch of a pair of male hands to repair anything from a sagging shelf to the most complex piece of space-age technology? And if a woman was to be so bold as to question their judgment or refuse their help, their egos were crushed forever.

Trying to hide her sour look, Houston got behind the wheel and turned the key.

Houston's car was ten years old. It drank a quart of oil a day, threw a rod every six months or so and got approximately eight miles to the gallon. It had never, in all the time Houston had owned it, started on the first try. Until today.

She turned the key, and the ignition caught and hummed so softly that, for a moment, she didn't recognize the sound.

"I don't believe it," she said, staring at the dashboard.

Mark's face appeared at the passenger window, looking just as stunned as she felt. "It's working," he said.

"Yeah." And not only was it working, it was working better than it ever had before. No hitching, no coughing, no misfiring. The car that only moments ago she was resigned to having to pay to have towed away was now running as smoothly as a Rolls-Royce.

She looked at Mark. "What did he do?"

Mark wore the scowl of one who did not like mysteries and had never before encountered one he couldn't solve. "Nothing," he replied.

Quinn closed the hood of the car and came around to her window. "It seems to be working fine now."

"Yes. Yes, it certainly does! Mr. Quinn—"

"Just Quinn," he corrected.

"Oh." His eyes, she noticed, were really more green than hazel. She found herself far too intrigued by the tiny lines that were etched into his flesh near the temples. She made herself concentrate on the situation at hand. "Well, um, Quinn, I can't tell you how much I appreciate this. I mean, let me pay you—"

He shook his head, making a small dismissive sound in his throat. "Not necessary."

"Well, at least let me give you a ride." And she smiled. "I guess I know how it feels to be stranded."

Again he shook his head. "Thanks. But I don't really know where I'm going yet."

"Do you mean you don't even have a place to stay?"

"Not yet."

Houston hesitated. She couldn't believe she was about to invite a perfect stranger into her car, much less her home. But that face... It was impossible not to like that face.

She said, "I'll tell you what. Why don't you let me repay you for your help with a home-cooked meal. You can make motel reservations from my house and call a cab or see about renting a car or whatever it is you want to do."

She could see he was tempted.

"Home-cooked?"

"Well, more or less."

"Mom makes good mashed potatoes," Mark volunteered, which surprised her. A moment ago she could have sworn he didn't like Quinn.

Quinn looked across the car at Mark. "Well, for mashed potatoes, maybe I'll accept."

And then he looked at Houston and smiled. Houston smiled back.

"All right, gentlemen," she said, feeling absurdly cheerful, "get in the car."

THE HOUSE Houston had been awarded in the divorce settlement had two mortgages, rusty plumbing and a forty-year-old furnace. It also had all the charm and eccentricity of any turn-of-the-century farmhouse, and Houston loved it absolutely. Buying that house was the only good thing—aside from giving her Mark, of course—that Mike had ever done for her.

It sat in the middle of what once was a huge cornfield, back in the days when farmers planted crops right up to their doorsteps. The cornfield was now a lawn that took an entire day to mow in the summertime, bordered by a former cow meadow on the right and a tangle of rocks and stubble on the left where, apparently, the former farmers had dumped the detritus of the fields they cleared as they went along. On the other side of that rocky, viny hedge were her neighbors the Barrys, who owned Arthur the sheepdog. There were five acres altogether, the perfect place for a boy to grow up.

The house was vaguely Victorian, with a wonderful rocking-chair porch and a turret-type window on the first floor where Houston placed her kitchen table. It had gabled attic windows and sunny bedrooms and a rock fireplace. So the ceilings were a little low, the doors a little drafty and the staircase narrow. The house had character, and that was what Houston loved.

And it was hard not to like a person who agreed with her on that subject.

"This house is incredible," said Quinn, running his hand over the door frame as they entered. "Are these plank walls?"

"Hmm-hmm. Someday I'd like to strip them down to their natural finish, but there must be thirty coats of paint on them. Back when the house was built it was considered tacky to leave walls unpainted."

He looked around the living room, the admiration in his eyes unmistakable. "All this wood," he murmured. "Can you imagine the trees it took to build this house?"

"Quite a few, I imagine. On the other hand, it's lasted almost a hundred years, and the trees that were cut down to build it would have probably been dead from disease or fire by now."

He moved around the room, taking in the paintings on the walls, the braided rugs on the floor, the wood chest she used as a coffee table, the lace curtains at the windows. Mark and Houston stood together, watching him, while Houston tried not to wonder whether he was casing the joint. It was the small-town mentality, she supposed; anyone else in the *world* would have known better than to pick up a stranger on the side of the road and bring him home, but try as she might she simply couldn't imagine that this stranger meant them harm.

He completed his circuit of the room and said, "Fascinating. Just fascinating. The best of everything this century has to offer, from beginning to end. Do you realize how lucky you are?"

Houston had to smile. "Well, yes, I guess I do. But I never thought about it quite like that before."

Heloise the cat sauntered in, plumed tail held high, and his eyes widened as he saw her. "Do you live with a cat?"

"Yes." Houston moved nearer to the cat. "Sorry. Are you allergic?"

"Why are you apologizing?" Quinn turned to the animal, bent down to approximately her level and said politely, "How do you do?"

To Houston's astonishment, Heloise sat up on her back legs, stretching up as though to get a better look at the stranger. She made a pleasant little mewing sound in her throat and, apparently satisfied with what she saw, dropped to all fours again and walked away.

Quinn straightened up and looked at Houston. "You really are lucky," he said.

Houston cleared her throat, still trying to rationalize the odd behavior of the cat, and said, "Come into the kitchen, will you? We'll have some cookies and milk and then I'll start dinner."

He looked surprised. "Do you have a cow?"

It took her a moment to understand what he meant, and then Houston laughed. "No, I have a grocery store. We only *look* bucolic out here. Everything we eat has been processed within an inch of its life."

And because he looked disappointed, she added, "Well, I do have a vegetable garden in the summer. It's too early to harvest anything yet, though."

He nodded and followed her into the kitchen. "You're obviously not a country boy," she observed. "Where are you from?"

And then she remembered he had told her that this morning, and it hadn't sounded like a big city. She took three glasses from the cabinet, then turned to look at him curiously. "Some place in Michigan?"

"Minnesota," he corrected absently. His eyes were busy taking in everything about her kitchen—refrigerator, stove, countertop appliances—as though he was memorizing every detail. "Clarion."

Houston set the glasses on the table. "I don't believe I've ever heard of it."

"You wouldn't have," he answered. And then he looked at her, his examination of her kitchen complete. "It was good of you to invite me into your home. Not many people would have done that, and I do appreciate it."

Just when she was beginning to work up a healthy suspicion of him again, he would say something like that, so unexpectedly sincere that as hard as she tried, Houston couldn't find a way to distrust him.

She poured the milk. "What do you do, Mr.—I mean, Quinn?"

"Do?"

"For a living."

"He's a field historian, Mom. He told us that," Mark put in. "Don't you remember?" He looked at Quinn. "What is that, exactly?"

As a matter of fact, Quinn did not remember having said that, and he couldn't believe he'd been so careless. On the other hand, when creating a cover identity it was best to tell as few lies as possible—especially to children, who had an uncanny knack for ferreting out an untruth no matter how well it was disguised.

"Actually," he said, "that's just a fancy way of saying I observe things about the times and record them for posterity."

Houston brought a cookie jar shaped like a fat orange cat to the table and removed the lid, gesturing to him to be seated. Her expression was interested. "What kind of things?"

"Everything. Things that future generations will want to know."

Houston sank into her own chair, tilting the cookie jar toward him. "Have one."

He did.

"So—what?" She still looked puzzled. "You're a writer?"

"Among other things." He bit into the cookie, whose taste was as rich and exotic to him as anything that could have been concocted in the finest of restaurants. The appreciation he felt was unfeigned, but he would, if pressed, confess to relying on it as a distraction tactic. "This is wonderful! What kind is it?"

"Oatmeal."

"I've never tasted anything like it. Did you make them?"

She looked a little skeptical, and he wondered if he'd overdone the flattery. "Only to the extent that I opened the package and poured the contents into the jar. What have you written? Anything I might know?"

"*A Social History of the 1950s: Cause and Effect,*" he replied without hesitation, reaching for another cookie. "Are you familiar with it?"

Houston shook her head. "Sorry."

Her skepticism seemed to have vanished—as well it should have. He had told her nothing but the truth. "It's not widely available." Also the truth. Although three hundred years from now, it would win awards and be considered required reading in every institute of higher learning on the planet.

"So," Houston said, relaxing in her chair. "You're like a sociologist."

He thought about that for a moment. "Like that," he agreed. "Yes."

"And you're wandering around the countryside as some kind of project for your next book, right? Society in microcosm or something like that? And this morning—the apple tree, the costume..." She grew excited as she came closer to explaining the mystery to herself. "It was all some kind of experiment, wasn't it? To get our reactions to the bizarre and unexpected when it happens right in our front yard!"

He stared at her. She had single-handedly and with no prompting from him at all invented a cover story superior even to the one he had intended to tell her.

"Amazing," he murmured. And then he added quickly, "I didn't think you'd figure it out so soon."

Houston looked pleased with herself, but Mark asked, "What kind of tools were those you fixed the car with?"

Adults could convince themselves of almost anything, if they wanted to believe it badly enough. Children were a much tougher audience.

Quinn began carefully, "It's not easy to explain in simple sentences."

Mark held his gaze. "I'm pretty smart." The challenge in his tone was unmistakable.

Quinn couldn't help smiling, at his own gullibility if nothing else. "I can see that."

Houston looked stern. "Not too smart for your own good, I hope. Finish your milk and get started on your homework."

Mark obediently did so, and then took on the look of innocence that only a ten-year-old can perfect. "Maybe Mr. Quinn would like to help me."

Houston looked embarrassed. "Mark, really. I'm sure Mr. Quinn has better things to do, and it's rude of you to ask."

Mark ignored the last part of her statement and replied, "Like what? Watching you cook? That's boring. I can show him my computer."

Before Houston could interrupt, Quinn said, "I'd like to see it, Mark. And please, it's just Quinn. What kind of system do you have?"

Mark got up from the table. "AT, forty meg running at twenty megahertz, but I'm building a new board that'll take it up to 120."

Quinn followed him. "What kind of processor are you using?"

Mark looked impressed by the question, and he seemed to warm to Quinn in spite of himself. "A 386. But I'm hoping with my birthday money I'll be able to upgrade."

"What kind of software are you running?"

Houston watched them go, amazed by the change in Mark as he broke into an elaborate description of the databases he had collected. At the door Quinn turned back, smiled and gave her an almost imperceptible wink.

It was settled. She definitely liked him.

Chapter Three

Houston changed into jeans and a long-sleeved white shirt, an outfit that some might mistake for casual working-around-the-house clothes—except that the shirt was carefully tucked in and the cuffs carefully rolled up and Houston never wore white to cook in. It wasn't that she was trying to impress anyone; it was simply that they *were* having company for dinner. And one should try to look nice for company.

In addition to the mashed potatoes Mark had promised, she made a meat loaf and a vegetable casserole, and actually caught herself talking out Grandma Perkins's linen tablecloth before she regained some perspective. She did, however, replace the plastic placemats with chintz ones and put fresh flowers—wildflowers, but flowers nonetheless—on the table.

Her efforts were not wasted on Quinn. The expression on his face was very near to awe as he and Mark entered the kitchen, and Quinn stopped. "I hope you didn't go to all this trouble on my behalf."

Houston was ridiculously pleased, which she of course tried to shrug off. "It's just meat loaf."

"Meat?" He looked at the dish on the table. "Do you mean—real meat?"

"I haven't learned how to make any other kind." And then her expression fell. "Oh. You're a vegetarian."

"No." He was still looking at the meat loaf as though he had never seen anything remotely resembling it before. "It's just that I don't get it very often. It's a real treat for me." And then he smiled at her. "Everything smells so good. How did you make it?"

Houston tried to hide the little skip in her heart with a laugh. What *was* it about that smile?

"What, meat loaf?" she said. "I'll give you the recipe."

He replied, with every appearance of seriousness, "Thank you. That would make a fascinating addition to my collection."

Before Houston could decide how to react to that, Mark spoke up excitedly. "Quinn knows how to design computers, Mom. He wrote a program that can automate every electrical system in the house—lights, stereo, TV—"

Houston lifted an eyebrow. "From fixing cars to collecting recipes to designing computer software," she said. "A man of many talents."

Quinn acknowledged her compliment with a modest bow of his head and a twinkle in his eye. "I didn't really write it," he explained, "just made a few modifications. But I do collect recipes, especially the good ones."

"Well, let's sit down and see if this one qualifies. Mark, did you wash your hands?"

Houston hoped she wasn't making a mistake. Since Mike had left she'd been almost fanatically careful about whom she allowed into their lives. Losing a father—even a low-down worthless scoundrel of a father like Mike—was devastating for a little boy, and Houston had no intention of bringing that kind of pain into his life again.

She had dated once or twice after the divorce, but it had been disastrous: she was awkward and the men were trying too hard and no one had any fun. Dating was far more trouble than it was worth, so she'd abandoned the effort. She had a few male friends from school, but Mark didn't like any of them. Sometimes she worried about the lack of a strong male role model in his life, but her standards for that position were high and she made no compromises.

Not, of course, that this man Quinn qualified either as a date or a friend—she had literally picked him up on the street, after all—and certainly not as a father figure for her son. But he was a stranger, and Mark was beginning to like him, and whatever else he might be, Quinn was only here for dinner.

As she served his plate, Houston asked, "How long are you planning to stay in our area?"

"I'll stay as long as it takes."

"Your project," she pressed. "It's fully funded?"

"Of course." He regarded his plate with a pleasured anticipation Houston couldn't help but find flattering.

Houston served Mark's plate. "By a university?"

He glanced at her as though he didn't, for a moment, understand what she meant. Then he said, "Oh—no, not exactly. It's more privately funded."

Houston didn't feel as though she could be any more specific without seeming inexcusably nosy about his financial affairs. She said, "Because I was thinking, if you're going to be doing your research in this area, it might make more sense for you to look for a small house or an apartment to rent in town than to try to work out of a motel room."

"That's a good idea," Quinn said.

But he really looked more interested in the meal on his plate than in accommodations for the future. Houston picked up her fork. Mark dug in, but Quinn hesitated, glancing around as though looking for something.

Houston took a bite of potatoes, swallowed and touched her lips with her napkin. "Is something wrong?"

"No," he said, and picked up his fork. "Nothing. I was just wondering—where's the cat?"

Houston lifted an eyebrow. "She generally makes her own dinner arrangements."

"Oh." Apparently satisfied, he picked up his fork.

"What about the garage?" Mark asked suddenly.

"What about it, sweetheart?"

Houston was still watching Quinn, and she couldn't help being gratified by the obvious pleasure he took in his meal. It was only meat loaf, but he savored each bit as though it was a completely original dining experience, as though he had never experienced anything remotely resembling the taste and wanted to commit each flavor to memory forever.

"Why can't he live there?"

The former owners of the house had built a small apartment over the garage. For a short time after the divorce, Houston had supplemented her income by renting it out to students from the junior college until she come home one afternoon and detected the fragrant aroma of pot in the air. The apartment had remained empty since then.

Houston looked quickly at Mark, then at Quinn. Before Quinn had proven himself to be a computer whiz, Mark could barely tolerate the man. Now he wanted him to move in. This was obviously more serious than she had thought. And it was of course totally out of the question.

Quinn met her eyes and she could tell he recognized her dilemma. He smiled and said, "This recipe definitely goes into my collection. Has it been handed down through your family?"

She recognized his attempt to change the subject and was grateful for it. But she couldn't take the opportunity for evasion he offered; she had always tried to deal with Mark more honestly than that.

"Mark, I'm afraid that really wouldn't work out." She turned back to Quinn. "I got the meat-loaf recipe off the back of a box of onion soup mix. My mother's not exactly the kind to hand down recipes—or anything else as a matter of fact."

"Why not?" Mark asked.

Houston looked at him, a little surprised. He usually didn't pursue a subject past the first no—unless it was something he really, really wanted. She was a little flustered.

"Well, Mark, it just wouldn't, that's all. The place hasn't been used in years, and it's too small, and it's a mess. There's no shower, and—well, it just wouldn't be comfortable for a grown man."

"I could clean it up," Mark offered.

For Mark, he was being positively obstreperous. But that was not the problem. The problem was that Houston was actually considering it.

She was actually considering renting out her garage apartment to a stranger she'd picked up on the side of the highway. A stranger whose behavior had, on more than one occasion, been a little odd.

She said, as firmly as she could manage, "I'm sure Quinn would prefer to be closer to town, Mark."

That was Quinn's cue to respond that he would, indeed, prefer more urban accommodations. Houston was a little unsettled when he did nothing but take another bite of mashed potatoes. When he did speak it was to say, "You're right, Mark. Your mother makes great mashed potatoes. Do you cook?"

Mark looked surprised. "Who, me? Nah, that's girl stuff."

Though Houston hardly approved of the sentiment, Mark was sufficiently distracted from his campaign to establish Quinn in the garage apartment. She was grateful for that, and was impressed by the subtlety of Quinn's touch... and a little sorry the subject was closed. That disturbed her.

"Is it, now?" Quinn asked thoughtfully.

Mark was a little defensive, but mostly curious—which only illustrated to Houston once again how difficult it was for a boy to know who he was supposed to be when there was no man to show him. "Isn't it?"

"Where I come from," Quinn said, "there's no such thing as 'woman's work.'"

"Where Mark comes from, too," Houston said. Turning to her son she added, "I can't imagine where you got an idea like that, anyway."

"From Dad," Mark replied. "He always said kitchen work was woman's work, remember?"

Houston clenched her fists under the table and counted to ten. When she felt she could do so without choking, she took a sip of water. Then she said, "Did you finish your homework, Mark?"

"Yes, ma'am. Quinn helped me. I'm finished. May I be excused?"

"Take your plate to the sink."

He did so, making all the normal noise of a ten-year-old in the process. He turned to Quinn. "Do you want to play some video games?"

"Thank you, Mark," Quinn said politely. "But as a guest, the least I can do to repay your mother for this fine meal is to help with the dishes."

"We have a dishwasher," Mark pointed out. "She doesn't need any help."

"Nonetheless," Quinn said gently but firmly, "I'd like to help."

Mark shrugged. "I'll be upstairs if you change your mind."

When he was gone, Houston commented, "You're really very good with him. You must have children of your own."

Quinn dropped his eyes. "No. I don't have a family."

The subject seemed a little painful for him, and Houston didn't want to pursue it. But she had to add, "You've made quite an impression on Mark. That's not easy to do."

He seemed to relax. "He's an interesting young man and I enjoy his company." He hesitated. "I was confused by his references to his father, though. Does he live here?"

"No. We're divorced."

He considered that for a moment, then nodded. "Who helps you?"

"I'm not sure I understand."

"With Mark. The rest of your family, your friends . . . the people who play a part in his physical and spiritual development."

She gave a little half laugh and a shake of her head. "If you knew my parents—and my ex-husband, for that matter—you'd know how ridiculous that sounds. We have friends, of course, but..." And now it was her turn to shrug. "Mostly it's just Mark and me."

He looked genuinely astonished. "But raising a child is the most important thing anyone can do. For society, for the species as a whole—you can't mean to say you've just been abandoned to do the best you can, all alone?"

"Well, I never thought of it quite like that before." And she didn't *like* to think of it like that, either. In fact, she was beginning to find this entire conversation rather strange. "I mean, it sounds great, and I suppose there should be someone—godparents or someone—who's responsible for that kind of support when the family breaks down, but I'm not really sure that would work in this day and time, are you? I mean, life is so uncertain—who can you really count on to feel that kind of responsibility for a child who isn't theirs?"

He looked at her thoughtfully for a moment, and she could imagine him quoting her in his next paper . . . only the truth was, it wasn't so easy to imagine his writing anything. He didn't look like a scholar. He looked, in his jeans and work shirt, with his tanned skin and tousled curls, more like an adventurer, a swashbuckler...

Suddenly she smiled. "I just realized who you remind me of," she said.

"Who's that?"

"Indiana Jones!" she declared. "It's been bothering me all day, and I just now got it!"

He looked interested but unimpressed. "Who's that?"

"You know, the movies—Harrison Ford—snakes, whips... I can't believe you never heard of Indiana Jones!"

He lifted his shoulders apologetically. "But I've got to tell you, if it has anything to do with snakes, I'd rather not. I hate snakes."

She laughed. "You are an interesting man, do you know that?"

The smile he returned was amused and secretive. "I'm not half as interesting to you as you are to me, believe me on that."

Houston was not sure whether that was a come-on, and decided she didn't mind if it was. It had style.

She gestured to his empty plate. "Will you have some more?"

"Thank you, I'd like to," he admitted. "But I won't. I'll keep my word and help you with the dishes, however." He picked up his plate and utensils. "Tell me about this dishwasher of yours."

Again she chuckled. "Just your ordinary off-the-assembly-line dishwasher. No, I take that back. It's over five years old and I've only had one repair bill on it. That makes it extraordinary, I think."

She swung open the door and started stacking the plates in the rack. He watched her with such intense interest that she glanced over her shoulder at him. "You *have* seen a dishwasher before, haven't you?"

The twinkle was back in his eye; his response was smooth and flirtatious. "I've never seen you putting dishes into one before. It's worth watching."

Houston's cheeks warmed pleasantly. That, she decided, was a come-on. But stylish.

He returned to the table for more dishes, adding casually, "If you have a technical manual, though, I'd like to see it."

It took a moment for her to understand what he was talking about. "On the dishwasher? Why?"

"I collect them," he told her. "Like recipes."

Perhaps one of things that most fascinated her about him was that she was never quite sure when he was kidding.

It took the two of them only moments to clear the table. When they finished, Quinn said, "If you don't mind, I'd like to take Mark up on his offer before his bedtime."

Houston closed the dishwasher and locked it, turning slowly. She hated herself for what she was about to say. She wiped her hands on her jeans and began carefully, "I don't want you to misunderstand this, but there are some men who might try to, well, get to the mother through the child."

His expression showed no surprise, anger or hurt. He merely said, "Perhaps I should just say goodnight, then."

"No, please, I didn't mean—"

He held up a hand. "There's no need to explain."

"It's not that you haven't been a perfect gentleman," she insisted. Miserable heat stained her cheeks. "I didn't mean to sound like I thought you were—"

"Don't apologize. You're perfectly within your rights."

"I mean, I know it sounded conceited and self-centered and I *know* you haven't done anything to make me think you found me even the least bit attractive..." She was wading deeper and deeper into a quagmire from which she couldn't begin to extricate herself. Why had she started this? Whatever had possessed her to say anything at all?

Quinn's smile seemed to echo sympathy for her predicament. "You didn't sound conceited, and if you had it would have been with good reason. And it's beginning to look to me as though I'm the one who should apologize—for not doing anything to make you think I find you attractive. I'd have to be blind not to."

With an effort, Houston tried to relax. The embarrassment that prickled her cheeks seemed to ease into a more pleasant warmth, yet her pulse skittered a little at the smile in Quinn's eyes. She took a breath and released it slowly.

"Forgive me," she said simply. "I have this tendency to turn into a raving lunatic now and then, but I recover quickly. It's congenital. All I meant to say is that I don't usually pick up strangers off the street and invite them to dinner, and the whole business makes me a little uncomfortable. Maybe I'm too protective of Mark, but I have to be careful. And I don't think he realizes that you're just passing through."

Quinn looked at her thoughtfully for a moment, and she had a feeling that what he eventually said was not what he had originally planned. "It's your job to be protective," he said. "And you should be careful. You live in violent, disordered times when anything can happen. And with that said..." He smiled ruefully. "I have a favor to ask you. Might I camp in your meadow tonight? As I told you this morning, I lost something there and I'd like to go over the ground one more time in the morning before I move on."

There was no way Houston could refuse such a simple request. There was no way she wanted to.

In fact, she was so relieved that she grinned and said, "That would be fine. Now, why don't we go say good-night to Mark?"

They were drawn into a three-way video-game challenge, with Houston trading off turns first with Quinn and then with Mark, until they moved up to levels that were too complicated for her to follow.

She then sat quietly in the background and enjoyed their interaction.

It wasn't so absurd, after all, to think a man might be nice to a child just to impress the mother. It had happened to Houston more than once and she hated it. But she should have known—she *had* known, really—that wasn't the case with Quinn.

He was nice to Mark because he liked Mark. He was nice to her because he wanted to be. And he was fascinating because he was Quinn.

He went downstairs while Houston helped Mark get ready for bed.

Mark said, buttoning his pajama top, "I don't see why you don't want him to rent our garage."

"I didn't say I didn't want him to. I said it probably wouldn't be convenient for him."

"Did you ask him?"

"And anyway, I wanted to talk to you about that. It was presumptuous of you to bring up the subject at the dinner table without asking me first, and a little rude. You put both Quinn and me in an awkward position."

"I didn't mean to do that," he admitted. "It just seemed like a good idea."

Houston turned back the covers of his bed. "Well, no harm done. Just ask next time, okay? We're a family, and we discuss things."

"Okay."

As Mark got in bed she added, "You like him, don't you?"

Mark's answer was carefully nonchalant. "Yeah, sure. He's okay. Kind of interesting."

There was a little clutch in Houston's chest at the reminder that Mark's faith in people was such that he could not even openly admit to liking someone. Much like his mother.

And Houston had to add gently. "Because he's a stranger, Mark, and he won't be staying for long. We don't know anything about him."

Mark took off his glasses and placed them on the bedside table. A small frown wrinkled his forehead as he settled back, pulling the covers under his arms. "But you know what, Mom? That's the thing. He doesn't seem like a stranger to me. I've been thinking, and it seems like I've seen him somewhere before. I just can't remember where."

Houston's frown matched her son's. "I know what you mean," she murmured. She only hoped that the place they had seen him before was not on a Wanted poster.

Mark shrugged. "Anyway, I just thought it would be kind of cool to have him around. There's something kind of strange about him—not bad strange, just weird. And it'd be easier to keep an eye on him if he were close by."

Houston hid a smile as she she tucked the blankets under his arms and leaned forward to kiss him good-night. Apparently Mark's latest interest was espionage. "Well," she said, "if it makes you feel any better, he will be around for one more night at least. He's camping out in our meadow.''

''Oh yeah?'' Mark looked interested. ''I didn't see any camping gear, did you?''

As a matter of fact, Houston had not.

She kissed Mark again, and stood up. ''Good night, sweetie.''

He had already closed his eyes. '' 'Night, Mom.''

IN QUINN'S WORK, there were certain unbreakable rules. There were the rules of physics, defining how and where one might travel. There were rules of technology that defined to a certain extent the comfort and safety in which one traveled. There were rules of ethics governing one's behavior in the past, and rules of noninterference that stated, among other things, the imperative for keeping one's identity secret and being certain to leave nothing of the future—particularly technology—behind. There were the rules of safety that dictated how long he could stay and how many trips he could make and how long he must wait between each one. They were all good rules.

In addition, Quinn had rules of his own. Primary among them was to never stay more than a few days in one location, because his time in the past was far too limited to see only one small section of what this incredibly diverse planet had to offer. And second, even more important, was to never form a relationship of any kind with anyone from the past.

Sexual liaisons were out of the question, of course, and were fully covered under Rules of Behavior for Travelers in Time. Applicants were carefully screened before being accepted into the program, and if they showed any signs of promiscuity, excessive emotionalism or a lack of self-control, they were dropped immediately. Moral implications aside, the psychological damage that could be wrought on the Traveler when he or she returned to his or her own time period could be devastating. This was easy to understand.

But no one had warned Quinn that the same dangers might apply to simple friendships.

The life of a Traveler was of necessity a lonely, sterile one. The choice was made when one entered the program. The Travelers were pioneers, trailblazers, the few and the chosen. They were also eccentric, self-absorbed and consumed by their work. Few were able to maintain friendships in their own time period. None had families, of course. They lived segregated, insular lives, forever set apart from the rest of society, and even each other, by what they had seen, where they had been and who they were that enabled them to survive. They were the heroes of their time, yet a surprising number of them succumbed to some form of mental or emotional illness by the time they were thirty-five.

The only real friend Quinn had ever had had been from the past. There was nothing more painful than awakening one morning to realize that the man you had been laughing and drinking with only yesterday had been dead for three hundred years.

Quinn did not intend to become a statistic. He did not form attachments to people from the past.

Yet he had been set down here in the middle of the most exciting decade in history and presented with the one thing he could never have, and it was hard, very hard to remind himself that none of it was real, none of it was his.

He had big problems—he knew that. He might well be stranded here, and he could only survive a short time outside his own time period—twenty-three days, to be exact. He certainly had more important things to think about than Houston Malloy with her bouncy red hair and rounded bottom that filled out the faded pockets of her jeans so nicely. Or Mark with his bright observant eyes and quick questions. Or this great old house that looked as though it had been standing here all these years, waiting for him to find it. . . .

But Quinn was an optimist. He couldn't have survived for long in his line of work if he was not. Every time he left home the odds were against his returning. The technology governing time travel was imperfect—as he had discovered for himself today—and there were still a certain number of grotesque fatalities. His field of expertise was one of the most violent and dangerous segments of history—the last half of the twentieth century. Every time he went back he took a chance on meeting with a fatal accident or random act of violence. He had long ago resigned himself to a somewhat shortened lifespan, and had learned the value of living in the moment.

There was nothing he could do about his predicament tonight. Tonight he could only appreciate the wonder of once again being in the most exciting century in history and think about the remarkable woman it had been his good fortune to stumble upon.

He was sitting on the front steps, watching the stars appear one by one in the darkening sky. Night fell quickly out here in the country, to the sound of chirping tree frogs and distant highway traffic. He felt a presence beside him and glanced down to see the cat, Heloise, regarding him curiously.

"Good evening," he greeted her.

She arched her back and made a trilling sound in her throat, to which he nodded. "I quite agree," he said, and extended his hand. She came forward and suffered herself to be stroked.

"My grandmother used to say you can judge a man's character by the way he treats a cat," Houston said behind him.

Quinn turned and saw her leaning against the door frame, silhouetted against the yellow light of the living room, an amused smile on her face. "And how do I rate?"

"Pretty high, in my grandmother's book." She came out and let the screen door bang shut softly behind her. The cat bounded down the steps at her approach, and Houston took her place beside Quinn.

She was wearing a perfume faintly redolent of vanilla and spice. It seemed to go through Quinn's pores like a tropical breeze. For a moment they sat in silence together, and it was a warm, almost intimate thing.

Then on impulse Quinn lifted his arm, pointing to a tiny star in the western sky. "What would you say if I told you that at this very moment, on a planet just behind that star, is a poet who is writing an ode to the light in the sky that is this earth?"

She looked up at him, her mouth set in an amused, skeptical smile. The ambient light caught in her eyes and filled them with subtly twinkling diamonds. "I'd say it's highly unlikely anyone on a planet behind that star could even see the earth, much less write an ode to it."

"I'm surprised by your lack of romanticism."

"It's just basic physics."

"What if I told you that in two hundred years that very ode would be considered the single most inspirational piece of literature ever written? A classic of its kind."

"I would think," she decided, "that's fairly likely."

He laughed. "You don't believe it was written, but you do believe it could become a classic?"

She shrugged. "If someone who couldn't possibly exist wrote a poem about a planet he couldn't possibly see, it would be more or less destined to become a classic, wouldn't it?''

Again he chuckled, but the laughter faded as he looked at her. "Do you believe in destiny?" She met his eyes. Her skin was pearlescent, her eyes dark pools. Her expression was thoughtful.

"Please," she said, "don't turn out to be a serial killer or a con artist or an escaped convict."

He lifted a surprised eyebrow. "All right, I won't."

"Because I'm about to do something very foolish." She drew a deep breath and pressed her hands against her knees, as though to strengthen her limbs. She said, "The apartment is sixty dollars a week, first week in advance. You can use the shower in the house, back hallway, and have dinner with us. Breakfast and lunch are on your own. You can move in tomorrow, but you'll have to give me a chance to clean it up first." And she looked at him anxiously. "How does that sound?"

"I'll clean it myself for ten dollars off the first week's rent."

She hesitated, then extended her hand. "Deal."

He shook her hand. It was warm and small and strong, and charged with a kind of electricity it was impossible to ignore. She felt it, as well, because she let her hand linger in his just a moment too long, then withdrew it a little too abruptly.

"Well," she said, and got to her feet. "That's that, then."

"Yes."

She hesitated. "It's pretty dusty, but if you want to sleep there tonight I can get the key."

"Thank you, but I'll stay in the meadow, if that's all right, and get an early start in the morning."

"Sure. That's fine." Again she hesitated. "You do have camping gear somewhere, don't you?"

He smiled. "I'm well provisioned. Don't worry."

"Because all I saw was that little duffel bag."

"I pack very compactly." In fact among his emergency supplies were all-weather housing, a blanket, a change of clothes, a climate-control unit and a personal computer. He did not think it necessary to fill her in on the details.

"Well, you're set, then."

She hesitated, looking as though she didn't want to leave. Quinn didn't want her to leave. But he couldn't think of a way to make her stay.

She smiled a little uncertainly. "Good night, then."

"Good night, Houston."

As he watched her go inside, his smile faded. He had a feeling he was about to break every rule in the book.

Chapter Four

Within a week, Quinn knew his plan was not going to work. The tracking device that would enable him to home in on the missing resonator was beyond repair. He was stranded in time.

If he had been the kind of man to panic, he would have panicked then.

He had visually searched every square inch of the area around the apple tree, to no avail. Without the tracker, there was nothing more he could do. And the part that would enable him to repair the tracker would not even be invented for another ninety-seven years.

He could try to build a resonator with the equipment he had and the materials of this century, but the chances of success were slim. He had never been more than fair in technology classes—though he scored high on inventiveness and creativity—and he wasn't entirely sure he knew how the thing was put together. He also couldn't remember which of the parts were indigenous to the twenty-fourth century, and which were currently available at the local Radio Shack. Radio Shack was a term he had picked up from young Mark, and though he had yet to see the inside of one, it sounded very interesting, indeed.

The sound of car tires on the gravel driveway distracted him from his ruminations, and Quinn went to the window of the tiny apartment to watch Houston and Mark drive up. It was amazing how much he looked forward to this time of day, when they returned from the school where Houston taught and that Mark attended. Today the sight of them saddened him, serving only to underscore the obvious: there was no longer any reason for him to stay here. According to his own rules, he had already stayed too long.

And the stars only knew he had gotten far too involved with this family.

The procedure, in a situation like this, was very clear. His first duty was to complete his mission, or as much of it as was possible to do, record the information for posterity and leave it in one of the designated "time capsule" drops to be recovered by the next Traveler. His second duty was to destroy all the technology he had brought with him from the future. The third was to leave no trace of his presence here in this century—not even, presumably, his own body.

The truth was, however, that the procedure had never been field-tested. Oh, there had been some casualties—some due to technical malfunction, some due to accident or illness—but in all cases the victim had managed to get off an emergency signal before succumbing to his fate. Never before had anyone been separated from his resonator. And though it was an acknowledged possibility every time a Traveler went abroad, no one had ever been lost in time before.

So procedures, at this point, were purely a matter of theory.

The car disappeared from his view as it entered the garage beneath him. In a moment he heard the muffled thud of car doors and the sound of their voices. He stood at the window, waiting for them to appear.

It had been a big mistake, moving in here. It would be a bigger one to stay.

Mark came out of the garage, his head tilted up toward the window. "Hey, Quinn!"

Houston scolded him gently. Quinn could not catch all the words, but it had something to do with Mark's bothering him while he worked. Quinn noticed, however, that she, too, cast an eye toward the window. He smiled at her.

She was wearing a rumpled blue skirt—she always came home looking far more rumpled than she had when she left—and a white blouse worn belted over the skirt, white canvas shoes and socks with lace on the cuffs. Her hair was caught at the temples with two ivory combs and spilled over her shoulders in unruly cascades of curls and spirals. The sun brought out colors in her eyes Quinn had never known existed before. She was so lovely, so delicate and natural, so earthy and real, that she took his breath away.

Quinn opened the window and leaned out. "Hey, Mark," he returned.

Mark grinned. Houston smiled and lifted a hand in greeting. "You want to walk down to the pond this afternoon?" Mark asked. "You said you wanted to see a real catfish. Bet they'll be jumping today."

It concerned Quinn somewhat that a boy Mark's age, with the opportunity to breathe fresh air and stand under the rays of the sun and taste the tender stalks of newborn grass, should spend so much time indoors, letting it all go to waste. Quinn had never seen a catfish in its natural habitat, it was true. But neither had Mark, and that was more than a shame; it was almost a crime.

"Sounds great," he said. He turned a glance that he hoped was casual on Houston. "Maybe your mother would like to come, too."

"Nah," replied Mark, "she's afraid of snakes."

Quinn rested his elbows on the windowsill, his eyes twinkling down at her. "Well, she won't be any help at all. May as well leave her behind."

Houston tossed her mane of strawberry hair and sent sunlight dancing. "Just for that I should let you go alone. It just so happens I'm the only one who knows how to call the fish."

"Magic?" suggested Quinn.

She grinned. "Bread crumbs."

The neighbor's big sheepdog came bounding across the lawn to greet Mark and he turned to race the dog to the house.

Houston said, "Come to the house. I'm making lemonade."

"Thanks. I will." He closed the window as she walked away, but stood there watching her until she disappeared inside the house.

His job was to record and analyze as much as he could about these last years of the twentieth century. In order to do that job effectively, he really should operate from a much broader base than Carsonville, Iowa. There was really nothing to keep him here. Except for the fact that lately it seemed the only thing worth recording about the twentieth century had sun-drenched hair and dancing eyes.

He moved over to the small chest of drawers that had been provided with the apartment, ducking beneath and climbing over the network of wires that were connected to, among other things, three television sets and two radios, all of them operating twenty-four hours a day. The top drawer stuck, and had to be wiggled open. Quinn got the drawer open halfway, then reached inside for the small packet of tablets. He felt the first cold clench of fear in his stomach as he looked at it. Sixteen were left. Sixteen days. It wasn't much time.

But then time, for him, had always been a relative thing.

He closed the packet abruptly and shoved it back into its hiding place, slamming the drawer shut with unnecessary force. His mouth was set in a grim determined line. There had to be a way out of this. There was always a way.

He just hadn't found it yet.

"I'M TELLING YOU, Mom, he's got enough equipment up there to launch the space shuttle." Mark gulped his lemonade. "You ought to see it. He must have a half dozen computer boards. And a palm-sized notebook computer that's really leading edge, I'm talking something *I've* never seen before and I've seen just about everything. And three—count them, three—television sets, all tuned to different channels."

"Elvis used to do that," Houston replied absently, wiping the countertop of the morning's breakfast crumbs.

"Who?"

"Elvis. He had a room in his house called the television room, and the walls were lined with televisions that he used to watch all at the same time."

Mark still looked puzzled, so she added, "I don't approve of you spying on people, Mark."

"It's not spying. He wasn't trying to hide anything."

"Still, I don't want you up there bothering him."

"I wasn't bothering him. I just knocked on the door to see if he wanted to play a video game."

"That's bothering."

"He said yes."

She gave him an exasperated look. "Finish your snack and change out of your school clothes if you're going to go trampling through the woods."

"Are you coming?"

"Do you want me to?"

He finished his lemonade and put his glass in the sink, affecting an elaborate shrug. "I wouldn't mind."

It was as close to a gracious invitation as she was likely to get, and Houston accepted in the spirit in which it was meant.

A week ago, Mark would have turned up his nose at an outdoor outing such as this. A week ago Houston would never have caught herself reprimanding her son for "bothering" someone, simply because Mark would have been too shy to boldly knock on a stranger's door.

The changes that had been wrought over the past week were subtle but definite, and when Houston thought about it she could not believe her good fortune. First of all, Quinn paid in cash, a week in advance, and the ceramic savings bank that held her secret stash of bills was growing satisfyingly full— and Mark's chances for a CD-rom were improving every day. Secondly, he had not turned out to be a wanted criminal or a professional con man or, as far as Houston could tell, a serial killer. And that, according to Millie, was nothing short of a miracle in itself.

Quinn had brought a measure of excitement into their lives that was difficult to explain. He carried with him an air of mystery and adventure and yes, possibilities, that made everything seem new. He was, for example, a news junkie. He read every newspaper he could find and listened to every news broadcast, and then engaged in lively discussions of the headlines with them, challenging them to stay sharp on current events lest he question them on some subtle point they might have missed. He spent an enormous amount of time at the public library, scanning periodicals, reference books and fiction alike with a single-minded alacrity that suggested he must be an expert speed-reader—and have a photographic memory.

He read technical manuals and instruction booklets—whether it be for a vacuum cleaner, blender, lawn mower or automobile—as though they were comic strips, and as far as Houston had been able to determine, there was nothing he couldn't take apart, figure out or repair. In the short time he had been here, he had fixed her VCR, her roof and a doorbell that hadn't worked since she'd bought the house.

Yet he seemed baffled by the concept of contour sheets and aerosol sprays. He had long conversations with her cat. He quoted haunting lines of prose by authors Houston had never heard of. Houston might have dismissed him as eccentric but harmless, or even filed him away under the caption "absent-minded professor," but it wasn't as easy as that.

There was an alertness about him that signified a man who had encountered danger and survived. There was something in the way he moved, the way he carried himself, that made him stand out in a crowd. He was good-looking, yes, in a very reassuring, guy-next-door way, but there was more to it than that. He had about him an aura of power, the kind of self-assurance that would enable him to deal with any situation, no matter how bizarre. Those were the things Houston had sensed in him when she had said he reminded her of Indiana Jones, and the impression had only grown more certain as she got to know him. Those were the things that, in combination, created a quiet strength and subtle sensuality that Houston, as hard as she tried, could not completely ignore.

She was glad he had come into their lives, for Mark's sake. And for her own.

She changed into jeans and high-topped walking shoes while Mark waited impatiently. She was just stuffing her hair under a cotton baseball cap when the phone rang. Mark answered.

Her heart sank when she heard his words. "Oh, hi, Dad."

A pause. Houston watched Mark's face light up as he heard the reply. "Oh, yeah? That'd be great! Yeah, sure! I'll see you tomorrow. Here's Mom."

"Hey, Mom, guess what?" His eyes were alive with excitement as he handed the receiver to her. "Dad's taking me out to dinner tomorrow night, then over to Camden to see the auto show. Won't that be great?"

Houston forced a smile. "Sounds like fun. Now go downstairs and see if Quinn would like some lemonade. I'll be down in a minute."

She took the receiver. "Hello, Mike. How's the new job?"

"Aw, it didn't work out. The boss was a real jerk."

Houston was not surprised. She pressed her lips together to suppress a sarcastic reply.

"I've got a lead on another one, though. I'm going for an interview in Cedar Rapids next week. District rep for Sugarman Foods."

Mike had no experience in either sales or management.

"Are you qualified for that?"

"There you go again, Houston. Can't you ever say anything positive? This could be a big break for me!"

Houston said with an effort, "I'm sure it will, Mike."

There was a brief pause, in which she could almost see his pout. Then he said, "Anyway, I thought to celebrate I'd take the little guy out for a night on the town. I don't suppose you'd want to come along, would you?"

And pick up the tab, Houston thought but did not say. "Thanks, Mike, but I don't think so."

"Come on, it'll be fun. Just like old times, huh?"

Every muscle in Houston's body stiffened. She had one of those rare brief impulses after which she was glad Mike wasn't there, because if he had been she might have done him serious bodily harm. She let a beat pass while she regained her composure, and then she said very firmly, "No, thank you, Mike. I have plans."

His tone was surprised and accusatory. "Oh yeah? What kind of plans?"

"Just plans. What time should I have Mark ready?"

"What?"

"Tomorrow. What time do you want to pick him up?"

"Oh. Five or six, I guess. Does that sound okay to you?"

"Fine. He'll be ready. Goodbye, Mike."

Lots of people have jackasses for ex-husbands, she told herself as she hung up the phone. *That's why they're ex. Just because yours is a jackass's jackass doesn't make you the world's biggest fool.*

But the sunny mood with which she had started out had dimmed considerably by the time she joined Mark and Quinn in the kitchen.

Quinn was leaning against the counter, a glass of lemonade in his hand, the open cookie jar at his elbow. He looked good in her kitchen—in jeans that stretched nicely over his hips and a cotton shirt worn open over a dark T-shirt, and with the sun from the window backlighting his finger-combed hair and painting bright planes and soft shadows across his face. She stood and watched him unobserved for a moment, appreciating the ease of his stance, the column of his throat as he lifted his glass to drink, the sound of his soft laughter as he and Mark shared a joke. *Why,* she thought a little wistfully, *couldn't I have married a man like that?*

She stepped forward quickly, before she was tempted to indulge in further pointless daydreams, and asked "Ready to go?"

Quinn emptied his glass and reached for another handful of cookies. "Provisions," he assured her with a wink. Houston couldn't help smiling. His sweet tooth exceeded even Mark's.

They set off across the backyard, Mark in the lead with a big stick "to scare snakes," as he put it. The two adults soon lagged more than a few steps behind, perhaps lulled by the heat of the sun and the lazy crackling of insects, or perhaps slowed by the weight of their own thoughts.

After a time Quinn asked, "Hard day?"

Houston hadn't meant to let Mike's phone call affect her mood, but obviously it had, and Quinn had picked up on it. She gave a dismissing lift of her shoulders. "Two more weeks until summer vacation. The kids are wild. No one really wants to be in school anymore, particularly not the teacher."

"If I had you for a teacher," Quinn said gallantly, "I'm sure I would never want to leave school."

She chuckled, carefully skirting a thorny vine that crept over the edge of the path. "If I had you for a student, I probably wouldn't last a week."

"I'll take that as a compliment to my quick wit and demanding intelligence. Still," he added thoughtfully, "it must be difficult trying to coordinate a curriculum for several dozen children at a time, all with different skills and learning abilities, all at different developmental levels.... It's a wonder anyone ever learned anything."

Houston shot him a quick glance, but had long since given up expecting him to explain those kind of off-the-wall statements. "You sound as though you have a better plan."

He looked for a moment as though he might tell her what it was, then changed his mind. He merely replied, "I'm sure someone will come up with one sooner or later."

"I don't suppose anyone ever mentioned to you that you have a...unique way of looking at things."

He laughed. "That's my job, isn't it? To put things into perspective."

"I've never been quite sure what your job is."

"It's not to pry or interfere in your private affairs," he answered, deftly changing the subject while appearing to do nothing of the sort. "I know that. But I wonder if there's not something else on your mind besides a classroom full of unruly students.''

Again she shrugged. "Ex-husband problems.''

"Mark's father?''

"Yes. Sometimes I wonder how anyone so utterly worthless could have had any part in creating someone as perfect as Mark.''

"He is an outstanding young man,'' agreed Quinn.

They shared a moment watching Mark, who was breaking a path before them in the high grass with his stick. Small though he was, there was confidence in his stride and a squareness to his shoulders that brought a proud mother's smile to Houston's lips.

"Have you ever been married, Quinn?''

"Marriage,'' he murmured. "An intriguing concept steeped in history and tradition. Sometimes I wish . . . but no, to answer your question, I've never been married. What's it like?''

"Marriage?'' She was a little taken aback by the question. "Well, it's not easy to say. I don't believe I've ever really thought about it in that way before—what it's like.''

She hesitated, wanting to give a good answer. As a teacher she was called upon every day to answer all sorts of strange questions, but this one came closer to stumping her than anything had in a long time.

"I guess—ideally, I suppose it's the most perfect union any two people can know. It's the closest anyone can come to actually being *part* of another person, do you know?'' And then she shrugged self-consciously. ''At least that's what I always thought it was supposed to be. When it works, it's the most wonderful thing in the world. When it doesn't, it's the biggest disappointment you'll ever know.''

Their steps had slowed as they walked, and Quinn was listening intently, a small frown of concentration on his face as she spoke. Now he stopped and looked at her and said quietly, ''I'm sorry you were disappointed, Houston.''

She turned to him with a flip dismissive reply on her lips, but it died unspoken when she met his eyes. There was tenderness there, and a glimpse of understanding that touched Houston's heart. She was not certain she had ever shared so much of herself with any man; she had not intended to do so with this one.

She didn't know quite how to respond, and she looked away uncertainly. ''We'd better hurry, or Mark's going to leave us behind.''

''He's lucky,'' Quinn said after a moment, ''to have all this open space to roam around in. Not many boys do these days, do they?''

''That's what I thought,'' Houston agreed. ''But Mark doesn't seem very impressed. He'd rather be inside, figuring things out, than outside roaming the woods. That probably comes from not having anyone to teach him how to appreciate the outdoors.'' Again she shrugged. ''Or maybe I'm just pushing my own expectations on him. I would have loved to have had a place like this to grow up in.''

"You didn't?" He seemed surprised. "I would have thought you'd lived here all your life."

She laughed. "Hardly. No, I come from a somewhat more unconventional background. And that's why I love this place so much, I guess. Everyone's a little reactionary when you get right down to it."

They came to a rusted barbed-wire fence that had been cut at the bottom two strands, forming a break just large enough for a person to carefully crawl through. Mark was waiting impatiently on the other side.

"You guys are really slowpokes," he said. "And you've got longer legs."

But he thoughtfully held the bottom strand of wire up for his mother to crawl through. Quinn, examining the construction of the fence curiously, helped him. "What is this?" he asked.

Houston looked over her shoulder. "What, barbed wire? You *are* a city boy, aren't you?"

"What's it used for?"

Houston got to her feet and helped Mark hold the wire up for Quinn. "Right now, nothing. It used to be used to keep livestock off the neighbors' property. Be careful, don't catch your shirt."

Quinn slid under the fence with little effort. "Are we trespassing, then?"

He didn't seem concerned, just curious.

Houston thought about that for a moment. "Probably. Fortunately, no one cares."

Quinn got to his feet with a little shake of his head, looking around with an odd sort of appreciation in his eyes. "You do live in fascinating times," he murmured.

Houston had learned to let comments like that pass her by, but Mark was not so tolerant. He pointed out, "So do you."

Quinn looked at Mark for a moment, and grinned. "Yes," he agreed. "I guess I do."

He placed a hand on Mark's shoulder, and the two of them walked together the rest of the way.

The pond was not very big, half an acre at most, but it made a charming picture surrounded by cattails and yellow and purple wildflowers. The late-afternoon sun cast a golden sheen across the water, and water bugs skipped like pebbles over the surface, creating ripples wherever they landed.

The ground sloped gently down to the edge of the pond, and Quinn took Houston's arm as they descended, their shoes slipping slightly on the slick new grass. Mark solved the problem in the way of boys everywhere—by sliding on the seat of his pants, and making it to the bottom in half the time as the adults.

"Hey, Mom," he called, brushing halfheartedly at the back of his jeans as he stood up. "Where's the fish food?"

"All the food in the world won't bring them to the surface if you keep shouting like that," she told him. She unzipped her fanny pack and brought out a plastic bag of bread crumbs. "Here. Toss these over the water. But you're going to have to be quieter."

Mark looked at Quinn. "Do you think that's true? Can fish hear underwater?"

Quinn agreed. "Evidence would indicate that underwater creatures can pick up vibrations—like voices—from quite a distance away."

Mark grunted noncommittally and opened the bag.

Houston watched as the two of them moved close to the edge of the lake, sharing the bag of bread crumbs, and once again she felt a little tug at her heart at the picture they made. And, despite her warnings to Mark, she was the one who squealed out loud with delight when the first fish broke the water, followed by another splash and then another. The excitement on Mark's face was wonderful for her to see as they pointed out to one another the pattern of surfacing fish, comparing sizes and antics, and the pleasure that spread through Houston's chest was warm and sure.

What she felt was contentment, she realized after a moment, for it was such a rare emotion that she had not recognized it immediately. She knew that she would hold this afternoon—the picture of man and boy, the sound of laughter, the sun on the water—secure in memory for a long, long time.

When the bread crumbs were gone and the fish returned to their natural resting place, Mark announced his intention of searching for water rats and started off around the pond. Houston chided him to be careful, then sat down on the bank to take in the sun.

"What is a water rat, anyway?" she wondered out loud as Quinn sat beside her.

"I'm not really sure," admitted Quinn. "But if Mark thinks he's likely to find one, he probably will."

"As long as he doesn't bring it home."

Quinn sat with his forearm resting on one upraised knee, his face turned slightly upward to bask in the sun. He pulled up a stalk of grass and absently twined it around his fingers. "This," he said in a moment, though almost to himself, "is a perfect day." And then he turned to her, shadows masking his eyes, though his expression was quiet and sincere. "Thank you for showing it to me."

"I could say the same to you," Houston replied a little shyly. "What started out as a really rotten afternoon suddenly got a lot better."

He smiled at her, and her heart skipped a beat or two. Then he looked away.

After a moment he said, "I knew a man who built a dam once. It was quite a project, hard, hot work dawn to dusk, but I never saw a man enjoy his work so much. When I asked him what kept him so cheerful all day he said, 'Just the thought of the day I'll be able to sit back and watch it fill up.'"

Houston grinned. "Sounds like an interesting fellow."

"He was," agreed Quinn. And his tone grew more thoughtful. "We spent a whole summer together, working on that dam. Those kinds of conditions let you get to know a man really well."

"Did he ever get to see it fill up?"

A shadow crossed Quinn's face; he looked at the blade of grass in his fingers without seeing it. "I don't know."

"Didn't he finish the dam?"

"I suppose so. But I had to move on."

In real time, the summer spent working with Sam on his project had been a mere five years ago; in the time of this century it had been over sixty. He had made three trips back to the same place, the same time, pushing the very limits of technology and his own endurance. That was before he had his own rules for emotional survival; that was when he had discovered the necessity for them.

Never grow too attached. Never grow too comfortable. He did not belong here. He was not a part of this.

He wondered what Sam, with his homespun philosophy and easy humor, would think of those rules. He wondered what Sam would say about Quinn's problem now, stranded in time with no way back.

But he knew. He could almost see Sam's slow grin, hear his lazy drawl. "Problem? What problem? Stranded in paradise with a beautiful woman? My friend, you've got to learn to start appreciating the moment."

Quinn looked at Houston. Her head was tilted back to the sun, her elbows supporting her weight. The thrust of her breasts beneath the soft cotton T-shirt was firm and round, a portrait of sensual allure that made Quinn's throat grow tight with need. The gentle dip of her waist, the flatness of her abdomen beneath the faded denim, the shape of her thigh... There was a great deal about the moment to appreciate.

As though sensing his gaze, Houston looked at him. He knew his thoughts were in his eyes and they brought color to her cheeks. The safe thing to do would be to look away; instead Quinn smiled at her.

He said, "Houston. That's an unusual name."

She seemed prettily confused, relieved yet surprised by the neutral change of subject. "My parents are unusual people."

"It's the name of a city, isn't it?"

Again she seemed surprised. "You've never heard of—?" And then she shrugged, apparently deciding he was teasing her. "It's the city where I was conceived, thus the name. Some sense of humor, huh?"

"I think it's charming."

"I think it's weird."

He laughed and she smiled up at him. Sunlight sparked in her eyes and washed her skin with clarity. The day was bright and full of promise and she was only an arm's length away.

And suddenly she was not. In a single unplanned movement he drew her into his arms and she seemed to melt there, a rush of softness and sensation, and he covered her mouth with his.

She tasted of honey and sunshine, velvet and heat. His pulses roared. She filled his senses, flowing within him like a meandering river, tumbling through his cells like a rushing waterfall, exploding inside his head with a rainbow of light. He heard her small surprised catch of breath, felt her sink against him, the weight of a soft round breast against his chest, the press of her knee on his inner thigh. His hands moved over her back, gathering her to him, and he felt the fine electric quiver in her muscles at his touch. She parted her lips beneath his and he tasted the inside of her mouth, devouring her, drunk on her, consumed by her.

And when she pulled away, breathless and flushed, with eyes as big as the sky, he had the oddest sensation—as though, in the few moments they had been together, less than a minute, really, something had changed for all time.

She inched away a little, casting an anxious glance over her shoulder toward Mark who, on the other side of the pond, was too absorbed in a trench he was digging at the edge of the water to have noticed what was transpiring between the adults. She looked self-conscious and unsure, dazed and excited. Her hands were unsteady. So were his.

"It's getting late," she said. "We should probably start back."

He didn't know what to say to her. He wasn't sure he would ever know what to say to her again.

After a moment he nodded, and extended a hand to help her up. "Yes," he said. "It's getting late."

Chapter Five

"It's amazing," Houston said. "I mean, we've only known him a week, but what a difference he's made. If someone had told me, I wouldn't have believed it."

"What I can't believe," Millie returned, "what I *still* can't believe, is that you, Ms. Ultra-Conservative, would pick up a perfect stranger off the street, take him home and rent him your spare room."

"It's not a spare room, it's a garage."

Millie arched an eyebrow at her. "A significant difference, I'm sure."

"Besides, he's not a complete stranger, at least not in the sense you mean. It's hard to explain."

"Obviously."

But Millie was right, and Houston was as baffled by her own behavior as was her friend. What baffled her more was that it had worked out so well. More than well. Almost too perfectly.

She was on a free period, and had started out correcting papers in the teachers' lounge. Then Millie had dropped by with a box of doughnuts still warm from the bakery and the papers went back into their folder, to await her attention at another spare moment.

"Well, don't you agree?" insisted Houston. "Can't you see the change in Mark? He's much more outgoing and interested in things around him, and he doesn't spend nearly as much time by himself. Why, only yesterday he led us on an expedition down to the old pond, and you know how he feels about the outdoors."

She tried to keep her tone casual, but even talking about yesterday made her pulse flutter like a schoolgirl's, and she was sure something must have shown in her face. For that reason she deliberately did not meet Millie's eyes, afraid that her friend, who could read her so easily, would see the whole story there. And Houston wasn't even sure what the whole story was.

"Oh, sure," Millie agreed. "Mark has seemed quite a bit more enthusiastic these past few days. Even Karen noticed it."

"She mentioned it to me."

"Have you talked to Mark about skipping a grade?"

"No."

"You should."

"I know. Karen wants to set up a conference next week."

"Of course," Millie added, disguising a shrewd glance with a nonchalant tone, "from my observations, Mark is not the only one who's been affected by this man. In fact, I'm afraid I'm just going to have to meet him myself. I'm beginning to think he's some kind of miracle worker."

Houston met her eyes, trying in vain to look uncomprehending. But she could feel her cheeks warming just from thinking of him. "I wouldn't go that far."

Millie broke off a piece of a doughnut—she was convinced a doughnut contained fewer calories if it was eaten one small piece at a time—and popped it into her mouth. "He makes you blush. If that's not a miracle, I don't know what is. Good heavens, you should see yourself. Your eyes are sparkling. That's disgusting."

"Spring fever," Houston replied. But she couldn't help grinning as she tore her doughnut in half, savoring each bite.

Millie's eyes widened. "Well, come on, already! I'm a busy woman. Do you think I went three miles out of my way for doughnuts just to sit here and watch you eat? Tell me!"

Houston laughed. It was a girlish, almost giggly laugh, and it wasn't a bit like her at all. When she realized that was how she felt inside—girlish and giggly—the laugh turned into a moan and she sank back in her chair. "Oh, Millie," she said. "This could be big trouble."

"I don't like the sound of that." But Millie's eyes were alight with interest as she broke off another piece of doughnut.

Houston thrust her fingers into her hair, tugging at the curls. "I don't know where to start."

"With the good stuff," advised Millie, leaning forward.

Houston encircled her coffee cup with both hands and stared into it, trying to put her impressions in order, and her feelings into perspective. "On the positive side," she began carefully, "you remember I told you he fixed my car? Well, he really fixed it. No more oil leaks, no more sticking gears, no more misfiring spark plugs. I haven't had to put gas in it for so long that I thought something was wrong with the gauge, but I had it checked out and it's fine. I figured it out the other day, and I'm getting *forty-two* miles to the gallon."

"Whoa." Millie sat back. "Keep him around just for that."

"He's brilliant, no doubt about that. That's why he and Mark get along so well together—they speak the same language."

"I sense a 'but' there."

"No," Houston said quickly, and then had to confess, "I mean, yes. A couple of dozen 'buts,' actually. He pays cash in advance, so he must have money—but he doesn't even have a car. No previous address, no employer—do you seriously think I could get involved with a man like that? That sounds like something my mother would do. I mean, the man is definitely strange.''

''Honey, you think all men are strange,'' Millie assured her. ''Not entirely without justification, I must admit.''

Houston focused on the coffee in her cup, a small frown of concentration furrowing her brow. ''On the other hand... It's not exactly something I can put my finger on, but there's an aura about him, a uniqueness...it's like, well...'' She glanced at Millie with a lopsided smile. ''He's got this enormous sex appeal, and he's so completely unaware of it—that's what makes it so exciting, I guess, so *natural,* and I mean that in the most basic sense of the word, almost elemental—''

Millie burst into laughter. ''You're babbling! My God, you've got it bad!'' And she clapped her hands together in delight. ''I never thought I'd see the day. I'd just about given up on you!''

Houston's frown sharpened, and she took a sip of her coffee. ''There's no reason to jump to conclusions. All I'm doing is just stating the facts.''

''And leaving out a few important ones,'' Millie said coyly.

''I hope you're not going to suggest—''

''That you're falling for this guy? The lady who has her life perfectly under control, a place for everything and everything in its place, who never takes chances or makes mistakes or even loses her car keys—that *you* might be going starry-eyed over a man you've known for barely a week, a man who might have fallen out of the sky as far as you know... Why, no, certainly not. That would be ridiculous.''

"It would be more than ridiculous,'' Houston said. She felt slightly hollow inside, as though all her supports had been cut loose and she was sent free-falling through space. "It would be disastrous.''

Millie chuckled softly and leaned forward to pat her hand. "Relax. It's only dangerous if he asks to borrow money. Up until then, have fun.''

"I'm not the kind of person who has fun.''

"So I've noticed,'' Millie said dryly.

Houston was thinking about his kiss, and every time she thought about it, that weak and tingling sensation began in her stomach, heat crept through her skin, and she could feel him, taste him all over again. And when she thought about it, colors seemed clearer, lights seemed brighter and she couldn't wait to see him again.

She murmured, "It's been such a long time since I've felt this way—about anyone. About anything. I'm not sure I'm ready for it.''

Millie smiled. "The best things in life are often unexpected.''

"I guess.''

"Come on. So you have a chance for a little excitement in your life, maybe even romance—what's so bad about that? No one's talking about anything serious here. I just don't like to see you close yourself off to the possibility.''

Houston didn't reply, and Millie added, "Sometimes I think you spend so much energy trying *not* to be like your mother that you don't have any left over to find out who *you* are."

Houston shook her head. "It's just—I have to be so careful, with Mark—"

Millie gave her a reproachful look. "Who are you kidding, Houston? It's not Mark you're protecting. It's yourself." And she added gently, "All men aren't like that rat of an ex-husband of yours, and that's all I've been trying to tell you all this time."

Houston smiled wistfully. "I wish it were that simple."

She took a final sip of her coffee. "The rat's coming over this afternoon, by the way. He's taking Mark to the auto show."

"Yippee. Does he know about your boarder?"

"It's none of his business what I do."

"Right you are. I can't help feeling though that that weasel would take off with his tail between his legs if he knew you had a real man on the premises."

"Oh, right." Houston tried to make her voice light. "Perfect reason to become intimately involved with a man I hardly know—to scare off my ex-husband." She lifted her shoulders in an effort at dismissal. "I like my life in order, that's all. I don't need some guy to come in and turn things upside down and inside out. I just like things uncomplicated."

But she knew in her heart things were already much more complicated than she had ever intended.

PRIORITIES. Protocol. Rules. They existed for a reason, and the reasons were valid. Quinn had always believed that—in a purely superficial, intellectual way. But three hundred years away from home, cut off from the chain of command and all that was familiar, with nothing but his own cunning and gut instinct to rely on, the rules seemed to have very little relevance at all.

He had always been something of a maverick; he knew that. But that was only because he was willing to take the chances no one else would, to push the limits when others backed down. In such a way were discoveries made, trails broken, protocols established. When they said it couldn't be done, he always found a way—because he had the insight to know when to break the rules and the courage to do it.

It was just a kiss. But already it seemed symbolic of every mistake he had ever made. And one thing was certain. He couldn't stay here. Not another day.

It was going to be inconvenient—not to mention expensive—to abandon his equipment and start over. It would also be time-consuming, when time was at a premium. But his first mistake had been in thinking he could set up a base here in the first place. Obviously, even then he had been thinking with his glands, not his head.

He needed to be in a big city, one with large libraries and industrial centers, preferably near a military base or government installation and within easy reach of a university. If he had any chance at all of reconstructing the resonator, he had to have help—databases, technology, access to the foremost minds of the day. He certainly did not need the distraction of a woman and a child taking his mind off his work, filling his head with fantasies, making him wish for things that couldn't be.

Of course, if he stayed, there was still a chance he might find the resonator. If he left he never would.

But he would be a fool to stay here.

He had given it a week. In that week he'd managed to complicate his life far beyond anything he'd ever anticipated. He had done his best. He couldn't delay any longer.

He looked around the apartment with a regret he had not expected to feel. The sloping roof reduced usable space by thirty percent; he couldn't sit up in bed without hitting his head. The bed frame squeaked and the mattress sagged, and there was barely enough room for him to walk between the chest of drawers and the rows of televisions. But he was going to miss it. And he couldn't remember what his living quarters in his own time even looked like.

But then his entire life had been a series of small crowded rooms in inconspicuous neighborhoods, base camps in a foreign land, one indistinguishable from the other except for the level of excitement, danger and adventure associated with each. Except for the one summer with Sam building the dam—a summer that, in Quinn's time, had lasted over two years of his life—he had never spent more than a month in any one place. He was always ready to leave, to move on to the next adventure, to make the next discovery, to meet the next challenge.

This was the biggest challenge of his life. Now, of all times, he couldn't afford to lose his edge.

Among the artifacts that were provided to authenticate him in this time was a man's leather wallet. It contained a driver's license—though Quinn tried to avoid getting behind the wheel of an automobile whenever possible—a social security card, some bank cards for nonexistent accounts whose only purpose was to further validate his identity, and—once Quinn had discovered it was traditional in this century for men to carry photographs in their wallets—several snapshots. Most were props, like the driver's license and the bank cards, but one was authentic. It had been taken with a real camera and the imaging processors of the time, more than sixty years ago.

It was a picture of himself and Sam standing in front of the partially finished dam, arms around each other's shoulders, grinning at the camera. Looking at the picture, Quinn could taste the heat, feel the ache in his muscles, smell the sunbaked sweat of other men. He remembered a time when he had been part of something real and important, a place where he had belonged, and the only friend he had ever had.

Sam had died in World War II. It gave Quinn an eerie feeling to look at the energetic, grinning young man in the snapshot and realize that at the time of the photograph, he'd had less than ten years to live. It was even stranger to know that, in truth, he had been dead three hundred years. And for Quinn it was only yesterday.

He had never seen Sam again, after that summer. He had begun to specialize in the last half of the twentieth century, and except for looking up the death record on one of his excursions into the sixties, he had not attempted to track Sam at all. There had been no point. But sometimes he wondered if Sam had ever looked at his copy of the photograph and remembered him.

He heard the sound of a car in the driveway, and instinctively his heart started to speed. But this time he didn't go to the window. He closed the wallet, and started to pack.

"HI, QUINN. Bye, Quinn!"

Houston heard the slamming of the screen door and Mark's first few running steps up the stairs.

"What's the hurry?"

"Can't hang out today—my dad's coming. We're going to the auto show! I've got to get dressed."

"Have a good time. Is your mother around?"

By this time Mark was at the top of the stairs, just outside Houston's bedroom. He shouted loudly enough to make her wince, "Hey, Mom! Quinn's downstairs!"

Houston finished tying her tennis shoe and left her room. "I'm not deaf, Mark." And then she tugged at her ear and added, "Or at least I wasn't until you started shouting."

He shrugged and raced off toward his room. "I'm wearing my blue suit!"

"Oh, I don't think—" She half turned toward him, but then stopped herself. She didn't think the suit was appropriate for an auto show, but Mark was so excited that she didn't want to spoil it for him, not even with something as minor as an argument over clothes.

Besides, Quinn was downstairs. Her heart had increased its rhythm, just a fraction, from the moment she had heard his voice, and it hadn't slowed yet.

She started down the stairs.

She had changed from her work clothes into shorts and a T-shirt, for the afternoon was warm. Quinn looked up when he heard her step on the stairs and she could not help seeing the smooth way his gaze slid over her bare legs, her thighs, her abdomen and breasts before reaching her face. It made her skin prickle with awareness.

She was glad to see him. It surprised her a little to realize how happy, in fact, it did make her to see him.

But these past few days, knowing he would be there when she got home in the afternoon, having him seated at the dinner table, had added something to her life she had not even realized was missing before. Maybe Millie was right. Maybe she should open herself up to the possibilities.

Maybe she already had.

She said, "Sorry about all the noise. Mark's a little excited."

There seemed to be, for just an instant, a look of sadness, and of yearning, in his eyes that startled her. But it was gone so quickly that she thought she must have imagined it, and he smiled.

"I understand. It must be quite an occasion for a young man to go out on the town with his father."

"More of an occasion than it should be," Houston admitted. "Mark's father doesn't see him very often. Come on out in the kitchen. I'm making a stew for supper and I need to start chopping vegetables."

Quinn inquired, a little hesitantly it seemed, "Why doesn't Mark's father see him often? Is he forbidden to?"

"No, he's just a jerk." Houston lifted her shoulders a little self-consciously. "And I have terrible judgment when it comes to men. I picked Mark's father for his charm and good looks, and by the time I realized there was nothing inside the man-suit except marshmallow cream, it was too late." Quinn was looking at her with an intensity that made her skin warm and her throat dry.

"The man is obviously a fool," he said quietly, "to have had the affection of a woman like you, and then not to do everything in his power to become everything you wanted him to be, and more.... He hardly deserves to be called a man."

Houston swallowed hard, a faint flush of undeniable pleasure spreading across her cheeks. Never had anyone defended her so eloquently, and with such quiet conviction, against so small an offense. *"To have had a woman like you..."* The implication was undeniable, and it made her feel quivery inside with uncertain anticipation.

Don't be hasty, Houston, she thought. *Think about this....*

"Listen, Mark's going out for dinner and I was thinking, since it's just going to be the two of us, and if you'd like, we could go into town and grab a bite, maybe see a movie or something."

She couldn't believe it. She had just asked the man out on a date. After all of her protestations about getting involved with a stranger, she hadn't even waited for him to make the first move. She couldn't believe it.

And her astonishment at her own behavior turned to humiliation when she saw the refusal start to form in his eyes, and the awkward way he responded, "That would be fine, I'm sure, but—"

"No, it's okay. Just a thought." Keeping her voice bright, turning away quickly so that he couldn't see the color scorching her cheeks, she opened the cabinet where she kept the glasses. "Do you want something to drink? I've got juice and diet soda."

There was an odd strained tone in his voice as he answered, "No, thank you. Houston, I need to talk to you."

She closed the cabinet, took a deep breath, and turned to face him, bracing her hands behind her on the counter. She said, "I know. I need to talk to you, too, I guess."

She met his eyes. It was difficult to do. "I don't suppose there's any point in denying that I find you attractive."

He seemed surprised but said nothing. That made it a little easier for her to go on.

"But I don't want you to think that I'm the kind of woman who corners every man she meets, or that I'm reading something into our relationship that doesn't exist. Yesterday..." Her cheeks were growing hotter; her heart was beating harder. She couldn't remember ever having been quite so uncomfortable in her life. "Well, it was nice, of course, but it was only a kiss. It didn't mean anything. I understand that. I don't want you to think that I misread you, or that you misread me...."

She blew a short breath upward, tickling the curls that fell over on her forehead. "I hope I don't sound like as big an idiot as I feel. This is embarrassing. Forget it. I never said a word, okay?"

With her hands upraised in a half defensive, half dismissive gesture, her face aflame, she turned back to the sink, intent on nothing except putting the entire humiliating episode behind her. With absolutely no warning at all, Quinn stepped forward and caught her shoulders, turning her to him.

Her breasts were crushed against his chest, his thighs pressed into hers. The grip of his hands was hard on her shoulders, and with her indrawn breath of surprise she tasted his breath, so close were their faces. His eyes were dark with passion. He said, "It meant something." His mouth covered hers.

The flood of heat started in the pit of her stomach and spread outward; the dizzying volatile chemistry of him seeped into her pores and suffused her senses. Helplessly her arms went around his neck and she tasted him, she inhaled him, she soared on spirals of powerful, single-minded, all-encompassing sensation.

She had thought, in the ensuing hours, that she had read more into his kiss than there had in fact been, that imagination had embellished her memory. But it was more than she remembered. There was magic there. It was crazy and she didn't want to believe it, she didn't want it to be so, but she could have happily spent the rest of her life there in his arms. She could have lost herself in him, drowned in him, become him. She wanted at that moment nothing more than to do so.

It took all her will to turn her head away, to brace her hands against his chest and put distance between them. She keenly felt the absence of him, of his heat and hardness and strength in every cell of her body.

His hands were on her back, strong, slender, competent hands that caressed her from shoulder to waist, that cupped her and held her close. When she tried to step away they were reluctant to release her. She could feel his heat again, could hear the deepened pace of his breathing even above the roaring of her own blood in her ears. It was with a very great effort of will that she turned and made herself step away.

The imprint of his touch seemed to linger long after his hands trailed away. Houston actually felt a chill where his hands had been. She hugged her elbows unconsciously, trying to mitigate it.

After a moment, he said quietly, "I'm sorry. I shouldn't have done that."

"You didn't do it alone," she said.

He was only a few feet away. Close enough that she could hear the soft, slightly uneven whisper of his breath. She tightened her fingers on her arms.

"This is going to sound crazy," she said. "If you knew me better you'd know how crazy it sounds. But that first day I saw you, in the meadow, it was as though—well, you looked familiar to me. As though I'd seen you before. Since then, it's almost seemed . . . inevitable between us.'' She searched his eyes, silently begging him to understand. ''I just wanted you to know that I wouldn't behave like this with just anyone, that I'm not coming on to you because you're a good-looking guy and you're convenient and I'm alone. I don't mean to be coming on to you at all. This is very confusing.''

His hands slowly closed into fists at his sides. His eyes were shadowed with pain. ''Houston,'' he said hoarsely, ''I'm leaving.''

She stared at him. The impact of his words hit her a moment later like a punch in the stomach.

He continued stiffly. ''I've behaved badly. I never meant for you to think . . . It was never my intention to stay for more than a week or two. I should have told you that.''

Why was she surprised? What an idiot she was. She *knew* better. That was what made her angry— not that he had betrayed her; he was just a man and he owed her nothing. He barely even knew her. But she had betrayed herself.

God, what a fool she was.

Mark clattered down the steps, caught the kitchen door frame briefly, and called, ''Hey, Mom! I'm going outside to wait for Dad!''

She tore her gaze away from Quinn, but Mark was already gone. The screen door slammed.

Quinn looked for a moment as though he wanted to do something or say something more. In the end he merely dropped his eyes and said quietly, "I am sorry."

Houston answered, "So am I." And she turned away.

After another moment, Quinn left the room.

He closed the front door quietly behind him and picked up the canvas bag he had left on the front porch, swinging it over his shoulder. Mark was sitting on the steps, dressed in a blue suit, with his hair neatly parted and his shoes polished. He looked around when Quinn came out.

"You going someplace?"

Quinn nodded. "I have things to do down the road."

Mark seemed unsurprised. He turned away with a shrug. "I didn't figure you'd last long."

"Why do you say that?"

His eyes were on the road ahead, watching for his father's car. "You're not the type."

That hurt. There was no reason it should have, but it did.

Quinn started down the steps. He lifted his hand to touch Mark's head or clasp his shoulder but changed his mind. He said instead, "Goodbye, Mark. It's been a pleasure knowing you."

Mark did not look up. "Right. See you around."

Heloise the cat jumped up on the rail, arched her back and made an annoyed sound in her throat. Quinn said to her, "Goodbye."

She sat down on the rail and stared at him until Quinn dropped his eyes.

Settling his bag on his shoulder, Quinn walked down the drive, past the apple tree, to the highway. He did not look back.

Chapter Six

Quinn loved twentieth-century motel rooms. He loved the smell, and the antiquated climate controls and the old-fashioned plumbing. He liked to sit in the restaurants and listen to conversations, or watch people come and go from his window. Tonight he would spend in a motel room. But try as he might he couldn't work up any sense of anticipation for what was coming up next. He couldn't stop thinking about what he had left behind.

It occurred to him that he was losing his spirit of adventure.

He had, of course, every reason to be downcast. He was all alone in a strange land, and the possibility was growing stronger every day that he would die here. He wasn't afraid of dying. He had faced death more than once over the years and had always emerged the victor. What he was afraid of was dying before he ever learned how to live.

The way he had behaved with Houston was unconscionable, of course. Some might argue that he had not technically made love to her and that the restraint he showed in not doing so demonstrated a certain amount of moral fiber. But in his position, in the broader ethical sense, there was little difference between a kiss, a seduction and a marriage—none were permissible, none were honest, none were *right*.

In the early days of time travel there was a great deal of heated debate by amateurs about the consequences of intervention in the past, among which was the possibility of a man siring his own grandfather—which was of course absurd. Some still thought that the strict code of ethics that governed the behavior of Travelers had its origins in those debates, but the truth was much simpler.

It required a lifetime of excellence, dedication and preparation to even be considered for the program. The screening process was stringent, the training arduous and the sacrifices severe. As a result, the Travelers were an elite, rarefied few, admired by many, envied by some, scrutinized by all.

Psychological weaknesses were one of the first things screened for, and that screening continued throughout a Traveler's career. Tendencies toward greed, megalomania or promiscuity were only a few of the reasons a man might be immediately refused license to travel, for any one of those weaknesses indicated a lack of self-control and a strong likelihood of developing ulterior motives for traveling back in time.

There were far too many acceptable ways to satisfy sexual urges in his own time. Any Traveler who attempted to impose his needs on a woman outside his own century was beneath contempt.

The strongest credo of a Traveler was to interfere with nothing. Their function was to observe, not participate. What kind of damage might have been done to the lives of Houston Malloy and her son had Quinn stayed, feeling as he did? What damage had he already done?

But perhaps more important, what had happened to him to make him behave in such a fashion? Where was his sense of duty, of self-control, of pride in his profession? Who—or what—was he becoming?

As the afternoon shadows grew longer and the rhythm of his stride became a comfortable counterpoint to the whoosh of traffic that moved past him on the highway, Quinn's thoughts took a more and more maudlin turn. He was growing obsessive, he knew. He didn't seem to be able to stop himself.

The first kiss was understandable, he supposed. Not forgivable, but understandable. His was a unique situation: he was stranded in time, faced with unsolvable problems and the very real possibility that he would never go home again.... A certain amount of disorientation was inevitable.

But today, after Houston had made it clear to him that his indiscretion had affected her deeply, he should have been alarmed, self-chastising, apologetic. He was all those things. But he was also pleased.

When he saw the flush on her cheeks, the light in her eyes, when he heard her stammering words, he realized that whatever her words might protest, he had affected her as deeply as she had him. Never before had he shared so singular an emotion with another human being. Even if what they shared was nothing more than surprise and confusion, it was, for him, a profound connection. And that was why, knowing it was wrong, knowing it went against every principle he stood for, he could not leave today without tasting her again, without sharing, in his own way, that one last moment of purest emotion.

And even now, having kissed her was not what he regretted.

The green highway sign said Carsonville, 4 mi. He should be there by the dinner hour, in plenty of time for an interesting evening of watching and listening, absorbing the ambience of the times while he mulled over his own problems.

Later he would begin investigating the major cities that would serve his purposes and choose a destination.

Quinn could operate a twentieth-century automobile in an emergency, but the rules and regulations governing their use on the roadways continued to baffle him, so driving was never his first choice of transportation. He did enjoy trains, though, and the gritty realism of being cramped into the thin metal compartments of an airplane several miles above the ground was an experience that simply couldn't be duplicated in his century. He would probably take an airplane to his next base. Unfortunately, there was no faster method of transport in this time.

Over and over he had pleaded his case for more attention to be devoted to finding a way of extending a Traveler's safe time in the past. Three weeks was simply not enough time in this slow-moving world, he had argued. And what if there was an emergency?

Well, now he had an emergency. Perhaps his untimely loss would speak more eloquently than his words had ever done of the need for more research in this area.

Carsonville, four miles. He would make some decisions then. He would, that was, if only he could keep his mind from dwelling on the mistakes of the past.

If only he could convince himself that the time he had spent with Houston *had* been a mistake. Because right now it felt as though the only thing he had done wrong was leave her.

He heard the sound of a vehicle approaching behind him and stepped over to the shoulder of the road and turned to watch it pass. It was a blue pickup truck, and as it approached it slowed, drawing to an idle beside Quinn. A man with a sunburned face and red baseball cap leaned out the window.

"Car trouble?" he inquired.

With most of his attention still on the house he had left behind, Quinn didn't immediately make the connection. "What?"

"Need a ride to town?"

"Oh. Yes. Thanks."

He moved toward the truck and put his hand on the door handle. Town. A motel. Tomorrow, an airplane. It was the sensible thing to do. It was the only chance he had to get home again, to put things right. He opened the door.

But what if the only thing he had done wrong *was* to leave her behind?

Three hundred years from home, maybe the only rules that applied were the ones that worked. Maybe this time he would have to make his own rules.

"You getting in?" the driver asked.

Quinn glanced back the way he had come. He looked ahead.

"No." He closed the door. "I guess not."

Some of the best decisions he had ever made had been on impulse. He could only hope this would prove to be one of them.

HOUSTON SLAMMED DOWN the receiver, biting her lip to hold back the curses. Mike still didn't answer his phone. He had obviously forgotten his date with Mark.

She wanted to hit something, to kick something. Instead, she closed her eyes tightly, took a deep breath and made her hand release the telephone receiver. She walked to the front door and looked out onto the porch.

There was her son, sitting on the steps in his blue suit, waiting for the father who had forgotten about him. He had been sitting there for more than two hours, watching every car that went down the highway. The part of Houston's heart that wasn't filled with impotent fury was breaking in two, flooding her chest with tears.

Damn you, Mike, she thought. And then, irrelevantly, *Damn you, Quinn.* Both she and her son had been betrayed today, by different men and in different ways. A son couldn't help trusting his father. But Houston should have known better.

She came outside and sat beside Mark on the step. She wanted to draw him into her arms and hug him hard but knew that would be unacceptable. She looped her arms around one knee and focused on the empty highway, consumed by her own helplessness.

After a moment she asked, "What do you say we go for pizza?"

Mark shot her a defensive look. "He could still come."

Houston swallowed hard but said nothing.

Mark's shoulders sagged. "But I guess he's not, huh?"

Houston answered gently, "It's pretty late, Mark. Something important must have come up."

"He could have called."

Houston had no answer for that.

Mark shrugged. "He just forgot. No big deal."

Houston managed a smile and squeezed his knee. "Right. No big deal."

Mark started to get up and then stopped. "What's that?"

Houston followed the direction of his gaze.

Dusk was deepening and it was hard to see, but a form seemed to be detaching itself from the shadows at the far end of the driveway and moving toward them—a form so familiar that Houston's heart started to beat faster even before she recognized it.

Mark said, "It's Quinn." The heaviness left his tone. "I thought he was leaving."

Houston said with difficulty, "So did I."

"Something must have happened."

"I guess."

She watched him draw closer, pack slung over one shoulder, stride long and easy, gaze steady. Her heart was pounding now. She wasn't glad to see him. She *wasn't.*

But when he reached the bottom of the steps and just stood there, looking up at them, she couldn't even speak, so many emotions were tangled up inside her.

Mark saved her. "Hi, Quinn."

"Hi, Mark."

It was difficult to determine in the dimness, but it seemed he was looking at Houston.

"You're back," Mark observed.

"Yes."

"Forget something?"

"In a manner of speaking."

"You staying?"

He looked at Mark, and the silence before he answered was meaningful. "For a little while."

Mark considered that. "We're going for pizza. You want to come?"

"Thanks. Sounds fine."

Mark stood up. "Think I'll go change."

The screen door closed. They were alone.

Quinn didn't come up the steps or even put down his bag. After a moment, he said, "I thought Mark was having dinner with his father."

Houston answered. "We were both stood up today." Her voice was surprisingly steady.

"You're angry with me."

"Yes." Angry, confused, elated, hurt, hopeful... Was there any emotion she was not feeling for him at that moment?

"I won't stay if you don't want me to."

"Why did you come back?"

He let the bag slide to the ground and came up the steps. He sat beside her, not deliberately close, but the step was narrow and their knees almost touched. She could smell his scent, warm and sun soft, like the end of a summer day.

He sat looking straight ahead, his hands loosely linked between his knees, and for a moment he said nothing. Then he said, "I'm not really sure. I think it was a weakness of my character."

She made a mirthless sound in her throat. "Why doesn't that surprise me?"

"Maybe it was just that—I felt needed here. I've been a lot of places and I've done a lot of things, but I've never felt needed before. I've never felt as though my leaving would make a difference."

"Well, you're wrong," Houston said sharply. "We don't need you."

He looked at her. "Maybe I need you. And Mark."

She met his eyes in a moment of confusion and uncertainty, then looked away.

He said, "I was out of line before. If you're worried I'll try to force my attentions on you again, I won't."

A half dozen replies formed in her head, but in the end sheer curiosity overcame the hurt and resentment and defensive pride she was feeling. She stared at him for a moment. "What *is* it with you? You show up here out of nowhere with no background or visible means of support, you fix my car, you put new shingles on the roof, you come on to me, you apologize, you walk out on me, you come back..."

She trailed off, exasperated.

He answered, "I wish I could explain."

"Maybe it's better you don't. I'm not feeling too happy with the male gender right now. I'm in no mood for lame excuses and rationalizations."

A faint smile softened the corners of his lips. "I wish I had a rationalization to offer you."

She drew a breath. "So. I'm supposed to just take you back in, just like that."

"My rent is paid until the end of the week," he reminded her.

Houston smothered a smile. "You've got me there." She glanced at him. "Any idea how long you'll stay this time?"

He looked at her, unflinching. "As long as I can. Not long enough."

Houston leaned her head back, releasing another long, slow breath. Of all the things he might have said, that was the only right thing, the only thing she couldn't dismiss... the only thing she did not want to hear. Why had he come here in the first place? Why had he come back and why couldn't she just tell him to leave? What *was* it with him?

The evening star was just becoming visible on the horizon. Venus, she thought. Or Mars—she wasn't sure. The god of love or the god of war; she would have to look it up—not that there was much difference between the two, come to think of it.

In the distance the tree-frog chorus struck the first few tentative notes of their nightly serenade. She remembered that first night, when she had sat here with Quinn and he had given her that wild line about poets in outer space. Had that been the moment she'd started to fall for him?

Without looking at him, she said, "My mother is...a little flighty. Well, some would say that's putting it kindly. You know the sixties?"

"Somewhat."

"Well, they were real good to my mother. My father, too, come to think of it. In a lot of ways, they're both still living in them. They never married, you know, which they can't wait to tell anyone who'll listen. She makes pots somewhere in New Mexico or Baja or wherever the latest spiritual center of the earth is. She calls herself Summer Moon and wears batik muumuus and turquoise jewelry. He's a mostly unemployed musician." She smothered a small groan in her throat. "Boy, did I marry my father or what?"

He looked startled. "Pardon?"

"I just mean my dad's a bum, Mike's a bum, and when I fell in love I was too young to see it coming. I think, no matter how smart you are, no matter how much you think you know better, people tend to try to be like their parents. I spent my childhood in a commune, not even sure who my parents were—until my grandmother took me home to live with her, and then I *really* didn't know who my parents were. My whole life was upside down. For as far back as I can remember, nothing was normal, nothing was sane. I promised myself long ago I would never do that to any child of mine."

He said, still not quite understanding, "It seems unlikely that you would ever take Mark to live in a commune."

She looked at him. "No," she admitted. "But I just might fall for the wrong guy—again."

Understanding softened his eyes, and with it came a quickening of hope, a shadowing of regret.

Then he said quietly, "I am exactly the wrong guy for you, Houston."

But even as he spoke he lifted his hand and touched her cheek. Her body responded without consulting her mind: skin tingling, heart pumping, anticipation leaping in every muscle. Houston took his hand firmly and lifted it from her face. But his fingers closed around hers, and she did not try to withdraw her hand.

She said, "I like you, Quinn. God knows why, but I really do. And that's why... I'm glad you came back. But I think it might be better if you'd stayed away."

"I think you're probably right."

But he did not release her hand, not immediately. And his eyes seemed to hold her with a subtle magnetic fire, kindling again the embers she had tried so hard to extinguish. With an effort, she pulled her fingers away.

He dropped his eyes and shifted his weight away from her. "I've never been as unsure of myself as I am at this moment. In fact, I don't think I've ever been unsure of myself at all before. I've always known just what needed to be done, and if it couldn't be done I found a way to do it. But with you, everything I do is wrong. Just believe me when I say the last thing I meant to do by coming here was hurt anyone."

Houston replied with a small shake of her head, "I don't know why, but I do believe that. I just think we need to slow down."

"I agree. And I'm not sure that's possible."

She looked at him helplessly and knew in that moment exactly what he meant. She could feel herself leaning closer to him as hard as she tried to move away; she could practically taste him now and feel his heart infusing her. He could feel it too; she could see it in his eyes.

Mark came clattering down the stairs, dressed in a T-shirt and jeans. The screen door slammed. "You guys ready?"

Houston stood up. "Right." She was more than ready—and more than confused than ever.

WHEN THEY RETURNED from dinner Quinn said good-night and went back to the familiar little apartment over the garage. He stood at the window and watched the shapes move against the lighted squares across the way, and he wondered again what kind of century this was, that a man could have been a part of so fine a family as this and then let it slip away. If ever he had such a choice, he would have made certain to hold on to it.

But that was just the point. He had made his choice long ago, and there was no turning back now. And his options did not include a twentieth-century woman and child, no matter how enchanting they both might be.

This was a hell of a time to start regretting his choices.

Even if there had not been a moral imperative against starting a relationship with her, even if the laws of physics had allowed him to stay, such a relationship was doomed to failure before it began. There were too many things he could never explain to her, too many truths he could never share. Where he had come from, the real nature of his work, the things he had seen and the places he had been that formed the man he was today.... He wanted to share these things with her, he wanted to take her into his life and become a part of hers, he wanted to try, for the first time in his life, to be a part of something that was real and lasting.

But the simple truth was that he could not. Even if he had not been just a visitor in her world, even if his home had not been three hundred years away; even if he had not made his choices and even if he was not a professional with a job to do—still, there was no chance for them. He had nothing to offer her.

He was dying. Day by day, breath by breath, his time was running out. He accepted that, but he could not ask Houston to do so. He could not make promises to her he couldn't keep; he couldn't give her time when he had none to spare.

He had been a fool to come back here. But try as he might, he couldn't regret it.

A shape paused before a lighted window in the house, facing him, seeming to look up at him. He couldn't see the face or even tell much about the form, but he knew it was Houston. He tried to clamp down on the longing that twisted in his belly, but he could not. He watched until she reached up and drew the curtain, sealing him out. Then he turned away.

He began unpacking the few belongings he had taken with him. The electronics he always left behind; in relative value they were so easy to replace that they were almost disposable. Tomorrow he would hook them up and start work again; tonight he simply did not have the spirit for it.

He took from his bag the packet of tablets, opened it and looked at it a moment before putting it away. One each day would keep him alive for another two weeks. And two weeks was not nearly long enough.

He opened his instrument pouch and took out a small cutting tool. Adjusting the blade to its finest edge, he neatly and quickly sliced each of the tiny tablets in half. Then, taking one half of one on the tip of his finger, he swallowed it.

It might not work. Even if it did, he knew he had only bought a little time.

For once in his life, time had become precious and he would take it any way he could get it. A minute, an hour, a day... It might mean the difference between finding his way home and dying here alone.

But every extra moment he could buy or bargain was another moment to spend with Houston. And in the end, if all he achieved was another day or two in which to watch her move, to listen to her voice, to see her smile—that would be worth it all.

When he looked at it like that, he really had nothing to lose.

Chapter Seven

Quinn entered the kitchen through the back door, which Houston always left open for him when she went to work, a change of clothes and a towel slung over his shoulder. Houston was cleaning the counters with a sponge, and he stopped short when he saw her.

"Sorry," he said. "I thought I heard the car leave."

Since there was no shower in the garage apartment, Quinn always waited until after she and Mark had left in the mornings to use the shower in the house. That was considerate of him. He always left the bathroom spotless, which was also considerate. But he had apparently forgotten this was Saturday.

"You did," she answered lightly. "I guess you didn't hear it come back. I took Mark to a birthday party."

"Oh. I was dozing. I worked most of the night."

They were trying to ignore the awkwardness between them, but it was as palpable as a humid day.

It had been almost a week since he had returned and in that time the atmosphere between them had been polite, guarded and strained. He took his evening meal with them and made interesting conversation on neutral subjects, just as he always had, and then he excused himself. He didn't volunteer to help Mark with his homework or play computer games. He didn't ask Houston what she would like done around the house. He didn't go on afternoon walks with them. He behaved like a paying boarder, just as she had requested.

She was glad. And she missed him.

She said, "I wish I understood what it is, exactly, that you're working on."

He murmured, "So do I."

She probed a little harder. "All those televisions, and computers—what do you do with them? I thought you were a social scientist."

"It's difficult to explain."

He still stood in the doorway, hesitating to come in, and it was clear Houston's attempt to ease the tension wasn't working. In fact, conversation only made the atmosphere more strained.

Still, he did his best to reciprocate. "Why are you home today?"

She smiled. "You *have* been working hard. It's Saturday."

He looked blank for a moment, then his face cleared. "Oh. Right. No classes on Saturday."

Usually, when he made one of those absent-minded-professor remarks, she would laugh or tease him out of it. Today she just nodded.

The silence lengthened, and neither of them seemed to know what to say next. Then he smiled a little and gestured toward the hallway and the bathroom at the end of it. "Well, if you don't mind..."

"No, of course not. Go ahead."

She turned back to scrubbing the counter that already shone. He left the room.

The relief that Houston felt was embarrassing. She hadn't been this nervous around a member of the opposite sex since she was thirteen, and the worst part was there was no reason for it. At least when she had been a teenager, she had inexperience as an excuse.

She found herself listening for the sound of the shower, and when it came, imagining Quinn pulling his T-shirt over his head, kicking off his shoes, stepping out of his jeans, walking naked beneath the steamy spray...

The sound of a car pulling into the driveway distracted her, and she turned toward the window. She only had a glimpse of the car and she couldn't make out who the driver was until she saw him ambling across the lawn toward her. Hands in pockets, head thrown back, whistling a carefree tune under his breath and swaggering like a sailor on shore leave was her ex-husband.

"Damn," Houston muttered out loud. The hand that was holding the sponge clenched involuntarily, squeezing out a stream of water that splattered her white shorts and her bare legs and caused her to jump back and exclaim again, "Damn!" as she brushed at the wet spots.

By that time Mike was at the door.

Quinn had left the back door open, and only the screen door was in place. Mike grinned at her from the porch. "Knock, knock."

Some women might have considered him an attractive man; obviously Houston had once been one of them. Now she looked at him and observed only that he wasn't very tall and his carefully styled black hair seemed affected, and the shadow of a beard that he thought made him look rugged in fact only made him look sleazy.

Quinn was always clean-shaven. She liked that in a man.

Houston looked at him, glaring, and said coldly, "You're a little late, aren't you?"

He looked mildly puzzled as he opened the door. "For what?"

Houston was surprised—not by his insensitivity or his ignorance, which she had learned to accept long ago—but by her own inability to feel anything except a faint disgust.

"For Mark," she said. "You remember your son, Mark? You had a date with him—last Friday."

"Oh." He didn't even bother to look abashed. "Do you know what happened there? That damn car. I was all ready to come over and the car wouldn't start. Can you believe that? It was the ignition switch. Had to go all over town looking for one, and by the time I—"

"You could have called."

He grinned and lifted one shoulder in a way that Houston could not believe she had once found endearing.

She said, "He waited for you for two hours."

"Man, I'm really sorry. Tell him that for me, will you?"

Houston's hands closed, and she could feel the tension winding around the back of her neck. "You broke that child's heart. What kind of role model are you, anyway? What kind of man can you expect your son to grow up to be when his father lies to him on a regular basis?"

"Come on, Houston, I didn't come over here so you could rag on me. Jeez, I had a better deal than this when I was married to you!"

She drew a breath for a sharp retort but the anger left her before it was spoken. She had long ago learned the futility of arguing with him. She shook her head and muttered instead, "Why do I even try to make you act like a human being? What do you want, Mike?"

Again he grinned, bad humor giving way to charm as it always did when he found it convenient. "Can't

I come see my favorite girl without wanting something?"

"No."

He pulled a chair out from the table and straddled it, arms folded across the back in another posture calculated to look disarming. "I miss you, Houston," he said. "We don't see nearly enough of each other. Can't we just spend some time hanging out, talking...you know, like we used to?"

Houston opened the dishwasher, added detergent and locked it. "We never talked. We never hung out. I've got a lot to do this morning, so if you'd just get to the point I'd appreciate it."

"I'll help you."

She stared at him. "Help me what?"

"Do whatever it is you have to do."

She made a sound of exasperation and disbelief. "No, Mike. I don't need your help. I don't want your help. What I want is for you to tell me how much money you want to borrow so I can say no and get on with the rest of my day."

He looked hurt. It was a look he had perfected over the years. "Money. Why does it always come down to money with us?"

"I don't know. You tell me. And while you're at it, maybe you could tell me why you never seem to be able to hold a job long enough to make your first child-support payment."

"Come on, babe, that's not fair. The market is rough, you know that."

"Well, do you think it's any easier for me? We're barely getting by as it is, trying to make ends meet on a schoolteacher's salary, and then you come along begging for money—"

"Damn it, Houston, I don't beg!" He stood up and pushed the chair aside roughly. "After all we meant to each other—"

"We meant nothing to each other, not for a long, long time! Why don't you just give it a rest, Mike?"

He ran an angry hand through his hair and then, with a visible effort, changed his demeanor and his tone. "Houston," he said plaintively, "don't you see what this is doing to us?"

"Us? There is no us."

He went on as though she hadn't spoken. "I'm a wreck without you, babe. And you just said yourself how hard it is for you and Mark alone. If we were all together, we could face anything. I know it."

Houston could not believe she had heard correctly. "And you think the answer to your problem is for us to get back together again?"

"Not my problem, babe," he assured her earnestly. "*Our* problem. We need each other—don't you see that?"

Houston didn't know whether to laugh or reach for the nearest heavy object to hurl at his head. Instead, she said, "What I see is a great deal for you, not so great a deal for me."

"What about Mark?" he persuaded. "A boy needs his father. I want to be there for him."

If he hadn't used Mark, she might have been a bit more tolerant. As it was, she felt a strong urge to start looking around for those heavy objects. "I want you to go away now, Mike. And I want you to stay away. Forever."

He smiled and took a step toward her. "That's not going to happen, babe."

Houston muttered, "That's what I was afraid you were going to say."

QUINN WAS SURE Houston did not know how clearly voices traveled between the walls, and he did not intend to eavesdrop. But from the minute he heard her say her ex-husband's name, he couldn't make himself stop listening.

He had an instinctive dislike for the man he had never met—the man who had disappointed Houston, deserted her son, caused her unhappiness and in general failed to live up to the definition of manhood in any century. Nonetheless, it was not his place to interfere, and he tried not to listen.

When he stepped out of the shower, she was saying something about money. As he toweled off, he heard the other man's whining, insinuating reply and he reminded himself of the danger—not to mention inappropriateness—of becoming personally involved in someone else's problems.

As he stepped into his jeans, her voice was rising and she was obviously becoming impatient. He knew he should move quietly down the hall and out the front door and let her conduct her life unimpeded by his good intentions. But then she told her ex-husband to leave, and he indicated he had no intention of doing so, and that kind of discourtesy was simply unacceptable.

Quinn started thinking about all the other rules he had broken since beginning this mission and wondered why he was trying to redeem himself at this late date. And as he was wondering, he slung his damp towel around his neck and walked toward the kitchen, wearing nothing but his jeans.

When he reached the threshold of the kitchen the man was half-blocking Houston from view, standing much too close, and Houston was saying in a cold angry voice, "Let me tell you what's never going to happen, Mike. You're *never* going to move back in here and let me pay your bills while you sit around watching game shows all day. You had your chance and you blew it big time, so don't come around here trying to charm your way back into my bank account. Because I'll tell you the truth—you're just not that charming."

"Honey, you know you don't mean that. It's obvious we were meant for each other. I mean, four years later, I'm still alone, you're still alone—what do you think that means?"

"Good morning," Quinn said.

Mike turned around, his expression startled, and Houston took the opportunity to move away from the counter against which he had all but pinned her.

She looked upset, but there was relief in her eyes when she saw Quinn.

Mike's eyes narrowed as he took in the sight of a strange man, half dressed and obviously straight from the shower, standing in his wife's kitchen. "Who the hell are you?"

Quinn replied, "I could ask the same of you."

The two men faced each other down for a moment, measuring, assessing, testing their territorial claims with a body language that was as old as the cave.

Then Houston spoke up quickly. "Quinn, this is my ex-husband, Mike. Mike, this is—"

"Quinn, I know. And you are ... ?"

Quinn did not know exactly when he had become angry. This kind of anger—righteous and primal in defense of a woman—was a new and satisfying experience for him, and he had no intention of trying to overcome it. It wasn't his place to interfere. He was going to interfere, anyway.

Quinn stepped forward deliberately and put his arm around Houston's shoulders. "A friend," he replied.

He felt Houston's surprised stiffening, but she didn't pull away.

Mike seemed to be struggling between belligerence and suspicion and finally settled for a combination of the two. "Oh, yeah? Well, what are you doing here this time of the day?"

Quinn managed to inject surprise into his tone. "Didn't Houston mention? I live here." He pulled her a little closer and dropped a kiss on her hair. "You should have told me he was coming over, sweetheart. You know I've been wanting to talk to him."

Houston relaxed against him, catching the spirit of the game. "I didn't know," she confessed. "Mike likes to... surprise people."

Mike was looking a little less sure of himself. His tone fell a little short of belligerent this time, though it tried. "What did you want to talk to me about? I don't even know you."

"Well, that's true. And frankly, I don't think you want to get to know me," Quinn said pleasantly, "because I really don't think we'd get along all that well. As for what I wanted to talk to you about, it's just this—the next time you feel you have no choice but to ask money from a woman who, thanks to you, is raising a child all alone on a severely limited income, come to me. You see, Houston can't afford to support you anymore, but she's too nice to tell you so. I'm not."

Mike swallowed hard, obviously trying to think of something to say and failing.

"And," Quinn continued, "although I personally find this hard to believe, I understand there are some men who would use a child to get to the mother. I certainly hope that's not the case with you. Mark is an exceptional little boy who can't help who his father is and who certainly deserves better than you. The next time you break a promise to him will be your last, so if I were you I'd think carefully before I made any promises at all.''

Mike's fists clenched and unclenched, the tendons in his neck tightened and his lips compressed. His eyes were a darting mixture of fear and indignation. ''You can't talk to me like that! Who the hell do you think you are?''

Quinn smiled. ''I believe we've covered that.''

''Well, we'll just see about that! We'll see what a *judge* has to say about that! You can't threaten me!''

As he blustered, he charged for the door, turning back with his hand on the screen to deliver some final stinging epithet.

Houston said pleasantly, ''Next time, call before you come.''

Mike pushed through the screen door and let it slam behind him with a bang.

The silence in his wake was weighted. Houston didn't pull away from Quinn, and though Quinn knew he should step away himself, he was afraid that doing so would only make the moment more awkward. Holding her was easy. Apologizing was not.

They heard the car start up outside and the spray of gravel as it left. Finally, Quinn said quietly, ''I know it was none of my concern. I heard you talking and you seemed uncomfortable. I let my anger get the best of my judgment. I'm sorry if I embarrassed you.''

Houston turned, slipping both arms around his waist, and looked up at him. Her eyes were bright—with tears, Quinn realized with a start—but she was smiling. She said, a little thickly, "Just when I needed a hero."

"Houston, don't cry." He put his arm around her, and she pressed her cheek against his bare chest. "I didn't mean to make you cry."

"No one has ever stood up for me like that before." Her voice was muffled, her breath hot and damp on his skin. Her fist lay curled and closed over his heartbeat in an oddly endearing way.

Quinn closed his hand around a mass of her curls and kissed the top of her head gently. "If I had a choice, you would never fight another battle alone."

The small sound she made sounded like a cross between a laugh and a sigh. "Sounds good to me. Oh, Quinn. Why aren't there more like you? And where in the world have you been all my life?"

Her words went right to the core of his soul. Quinn took a long deep breath, drawing in the scent of her, the essence of her. Spice and vanilla. He would never forget it. It would float inside his head, haunting his dreams and his silent moments for all eternity.

She stepped away, looking up at him with a little smile of regret and gratitude. The flesh around her eyes was damp, but the tears were gone, leaving only a sweet rosiness about her nose and cheeks. Before he could stop himself he leaned down and tenderly kissed the corner of her eyes where teardrops had stained.

He straightened up slowly, tasting salt and softness. She did not move, but watched him with quiet, star-bright eyes. The moment seemed to be suspended between them, heartbeats, breaths. Waiting... but for what, neither one would say, even to themselves.

Quinn said, "I'd better go."

She said nothing. He could see the slow rise and fall of her breast and feel the heavy pounding of his heart. Her hands were on his back, near his waist, her fingers against his waistband, the curve of her thumbs brushing his skin. Every muscle in his body tightened with awareness, and even his pores seemed to expand, taking her in.

His voice dropped just a fraction in timbre. "I've been impulsive once today."

And she replied, "That didn't work out so badly, did it?"

Her eyes were big and searching, asking but not answering. All he could think about was holding her.

"Houston." His hands slid up her back almost as though they were controlled by a power greater than his own will. "I thought we had agreed."

"On what?"

"This isn't good... for either of us." But her face was so close, her breath so warm and her lips so soft and moist that he leaned forward and tasted her, softly breathing into her. "You make it hard to think."

"Don't think," she whispered.

"Houston..."

Her fingers curved inside his waistband. Her eyes were heavy lidded, her face faintly flushed. "I'm never impulsive, Quinn. I think I should be...just this once."

His muscles ached with trying to keep from crushing her against him; wanting her actually hurt, deep inside his skin. He said, "Houston, don't." But he could not make his body obey the command of his words. He could not make himself step away. He couldn't even make himself look away. He wanted to draw her closer and closer still; he wanted to drown in her closeness.

"I want to be your lover," she whispered.

He said hoarsely, "That's...not possible." But nothing had ever seemed more possible, more right, more real.

Her breath was quick, and he imagined he could feel the beat of her heart, fast and strong, against his. "It's possible," she said. "It's crazy, it's dangerous, it's wrong...but it's possible. And you want it, too."

"Yes."

"Now...we just have to decide what we're going to do about it."

"Nothing," he said. "We're going to do nothing."

And then he drew her into his arms and covered her mouth with his and he was lost in her, suffused with her, drowning in her. Her mouth opened beneath his, he felt the press of her tongue and the sweet tangy taste of her, her hand on his face and in his hair. His head spun. He tried to remember all the reasons this was wrong. He could remember nothing, not his past, not the future, not the rules. Least of all the rules.

It had been so long since Houston had been held like this, with power and purpose, been drunk on a man's kisses, felt the very blood in her veins ignite her senses and known the promise of what was to come.... So long. Too long. And never had it been this potent, this mind robbing, this insistent. For every cell in her body, every sensory ending and nerve fiber demanded him, insisted on him, could not continue to exist without him.

She wasn't impulsive. She wasn't reckless or careless like her mother. But Quinn was more than an impulse, he had been since the moment she had first seen him. He was her destiny.

They parted for breath and the room was bright and feverish, pulsing in an odd and wonderful way. His face was close to hers, flushed with passion, dark with desire. She wound her fingers through his and whispered, "Come with me."

She led him to the bedroom with its sun-splashed walls and dark polished floors, its white cotton counterpane and peach striped sheets still faintly scented with the warmth of her sleep. She closed the door and turned to him.

He stepped close, almost touching, embracing her with a promise rather than in fact. His eyes were dark and alive, his face wonderfully strong, wonderfully familiar. His hands were poised on either side of her shoulders, a mere breath away. "Don't be sorry," he said huskily. "Don't . . . be wrong."

It was hard to talk, her throat ached so. But she knew the words had to be said. "If . . . you leave me, or hurt me, or betray me . . . I'll be sad. But I won't be sorry."

A shadow of pain darkened his eyes. His hands cupped her shoulders ever so lightly, barely touching at all, yet communicating a universe of emotion with his touch. "I will do all those things." His voice was strained. "Please understand, Houston. I can't stay. I will leave you. It may be today, it may be tomorrow . . . but I will leave. I have no promises to make, nothing to give you . . . except this moment."

"That's all I ask," she whispered.

His hands slid down, arms embracing her, cradling her against his chest. She opened her mouth, inhaling his fragrance, tasting the smooth heat of his chest with the tip of her tongue. She could feel the strength of his arousal, separated from her only by the thin layers of their clothes, the tightness of his muscles, the fan of his breath, hot and strong on her face. His fingers tangled in her hair, and he pressed a kiss against her neck. Her knees went weak. Nothing had ever felt so right. Nothing.

They sank to the bed in a slow-motion turn, splashed with sunlight and swirling colors. Their clothes came off and Houston did not remember how; she only knew the sensation of warm bare skin against bare skin, of muscles and ridges, planes and curves. Pleasure and need flowed into one another and if there were any lingering doubts or uncertainties they spiraled away on the morning breeze.

They melted into each other, as though they had always belonged together, their bodies perfectly fitted, hearts perfectly synchronized. Houston gave herself over to sensation, thoroughly awash in it, completely lost. His skin, hot and slippery beneath her fingers. The exquisite waves of pleasure generated by his mouth on her breasts, his fingers on her thigh. The low rush of his breath mingling with her own, the pounding of heartbeats. And the sharp aching pleasure of his entry, filling her, melding with her, becoming a part of her as she was of him.

She watched his face and let him see hers as they came together—with intensity and desire, pleasure and wonder, tenderness and care. His hands cupped her face, smoothed back her damp tangled curls. He kissed her eyelids, and her cheeks. She wrapped her legs around him, drawing him deep within her, holding him there, arching into him. She felt his response in every muscle, in his breath and pulse and even in his skin. His pleasure was hers and hers his.

They moved together in perfect rhythm, letting the love they made carry them to its own predestined peak. It was as though something outside them both had taken over, cradling them in its embrace, weaving the threads of trust and harmony into a silken web that bound them both. And when the pinnacle of pleasure was reached it cascaded around and through them in undulant waves, and they clung together helplessly, suspended in emotion, until they came to rest in each other's arms.

Time stopped. Quinn measured the passing of minutes by the pace of his breathing, but even his breath seemed to flow into hers, leaving nothing separate unto himself anymore, nothing that mattered outside of her. The sun sparkling on her hair. The curve of her shoulder, sheened with perspiration. The rise and fall of her chest with each breath.

She lay on her side with her cheek cradled in the curve of his arm, tangled in peach striped sheets and his embrace. He looked at her and his heart ached. *Now,* he thought, *I've done everything. Broken every rule, flouted every law.* He wondered what became of a man when he turned his back even on his own code of ethics.

He tried to summon regret. He could not.

He understood the morals of her century, and they were different from his own. It was not uncommon in this time for a man and a woman to share this most intimate of human experiences as casually as they might exchange a handshake and walk away unchanged. In this time, sexual encounters were for the most part meaningless, having to do more with recreation than with emotion. For that he should have been grateful.

But he could not make what they had just shared meaningless. And he did not think Houston could, either.

She raised her face to him and smiled. "I wish I knew what you were thinking," she said softly.

He brushed a strand of hair away from her mouth. "Weighty moral issues," he replied, twisting the strand around his finger. "Dull stuff."

She laughed softly, her eyes taking on the sparkle that he loved. "You are a very unusual man, Quinn," she said.

And then the laughter faded into uncertainty, a shy and gentle curiosity as though, even after all they had shared, she wasn't sure she had the right to ask the question. "What is back in Clarion, Minnesota, that is going to take you away from me?"

He said, puzzled, "Where?"

"Clarion, Minnesota. That's where you're from, isn't it?"

He relaxed. "That's where I was born. It's not where I work."

"Where do you work?"

He thought about the place so far in the future that it could not even be called a city, its name a word that wasn't even a part of the language yet. Thinking about it made him sad. He could leave her nothing, not even a picture of him in her head in the place where he belonged. He said, "You wouldn't have heard of it."

She shifted her position, her head still on his shoulder, eyes toward the ceiling. He could feel some of the easy closeness between them slip away. "This isn't easy for me," she said. "Sleeping with a man I don't know. I'm trying but . . . it's not easy."

His arms tightened around her instinctively. He had not thought before what a simple act of courage it had been for her to surrender to her emotions and share this moment with him. He was a stranger to her, a mystery, maybe dangerous, always uncertain. He had walked away from her once, just as her husband had, and had all but promised to do it again. Yet she had opened herself to him.

How could he not love her for that?

He kissed her forehead, his heart beating slow and hard. "I don't want it to be easy for you," he said. "If it were, you wouldn't be Houston."

He lay back against the pillow, holding her. He gazed at the ceiling, just as she did. "I wish I could tell you more. I wish I could tell you everything. Most of it you wouldn't believe, parts of it you wouldn't understand—but I wish I could tell you, anyway."

She inquired hesitantly, "Do you work for the government? Are you some kind of . . . agent?"

He smiled. "Do you mean spy? No. It's nothing like that."

"I don't mean to sound silly. A lot of guys would have gone with the old 'CIA agent' line, though, once I offered it to them."

"Maybe I should have."

"No," she answered seriously. "Don't lie. Not if you can help it. Please."

He turned his head on the pillow and found her looking at him. He curled his fingers against her cheek. "That I promise."

"Do you think..." She swallowed. Her eyes searched his. "Do you think you'll ever tell me?"

He had broken all the other rules. Would it really mean so much to break one more?

He answered as honestly as he could, "I don't know. I don't think so."

She dropped her eyes, her struggle to accept this apparent. Then she said, "Could I ask you one more question?"

He nodded, his chin brushing the top of her head.

She glanced up at him. "Your name. Is Quinn your first name or last?"

He hesitated, then smiled. "On my driver's license it says, 'David Quinn'. But my name is just Quinn."

"David." She repeated the word softly. Then she smiled, though it seemed a little sad. "That's something, at least."

"I wish I could give you more. I wish..." He felt his chest tighten with the intensity of that wish. "I would give all that I know not to be the one to cause you pain.''

"Oh, Quinn."

She turned to him, arms sliding around him, legs encircling his. Her eyes were clear and quiet and gentle. "Look at me. I'm not sorry. Whatever else happens, you've given me something I'll treasure forever. You've shown me something about myself I can fall back on whenever I need it. I wasn't sure I'd ever know what I've just shared with you and that's a good thing. I'm not sorry."

He kissed her, savoring her, treasuring her, wishing for more. Wishing for forever.

He said into her hair, "Why did we do this, Houston? We're both wise enough to know better. It can only get more complicated from here."

"I told you I wouldn't be sorry."

He answered quietly, "I made you no such promise."

Her fingers entwined with his as though their symbolic unity was enough to defy the consequences that must now be faced. She didn't look at him when she spoke, and her voice was low. "I should probably say something about how it doesn't matter if I never see you again and I never wanted anything more than this one time with you and I never expected this to lead to anything more permanent. . . . And all of that's true. And it's not. I could fall in love with you, Quinn. And it scares the hell out of me."

He tightened his fingers around hers. He didn't know what to say. It would be unfair of him to speak what was in his heart, because he didn't know his heart anymore. He had never thought he was capable of feelings such as this, not with a twentieth-century woman—not with anyone at all. But he didn't want to say that. He couldn't offer her hope when he knew there was no hope for them, as much as he might wish it could be different. With all his being he wished he could be a twentieth-century man and that he could say to her the words she needed to hear, make her the promises she deserved to have.

But all he could say was, softly, "It was more than just making love for me. Please believe that."

She nodded against his shoulder, slowly. She was so trusting, so gentle. His heart ached for her.

After a moment, she said softly, "Do you believe in destiny, Quinn?"

He thought about it, wishing he could give her the answer she wanted. "No," he admitted. "I've seen too much evidence to the contrary. We make our own destinies, for good or bad."

"I think you're wrong. I didn't used to believe, either, but since I met you...now I think you're wrong."

"What do you think destiny has in store for us, then?"

She was silent for a moment, and he thought she was formulating a reply. But in the end she merely smiled a little and shook her head.

"Maybe you're right. Maybe there's no such thing."

"Or maybe," he suggested, "it's best not to know."

She caressed his cheek. "I have to go pick up Mark in an hour," she said. "We may not be able to be together like this again."

He nodded.

"For now . . . would you just hold me?"

He drew her into his arms and wrapped her in the cocoon of his legs, and he held her.

And while he did, a solution began to occur to him.

Chapter Eight

Quinn had to get back home. It was as simple as that.

The project that had once been urgent was now imperative. Once only his life had been at stake, but Quinn was prepared to lose his life; he had been from the moment he started training for the program. Travelers lived lives charged with danger and excitement, and they died young. Everyone knew that. To lose a life in the performance of one's duty was neither a surprise nor a sacrifice.

But now he had found something worth living for, and that added an immediacy to his need, determination to his plan. He had to get home. Only by doing so could he stay with Houston, and give them each the time they needed to allow what had begun between them to grow and flourish. And if all went according to his plan, she would never even know he was gone.

If all went according to plan, he would never have to leave her again.

His plan was reckless, renegade, wild in the extreme. If he succeeded, some might say he would have lost more than he gained. He would be a fugitive in time, unable to return home again, a disgrace to his profession and a blight on the history books. And all this for the sake of a twentieth-century woman. It was absurd. But some might say it was fate.

Before there had been only the need, but now there was real hope. It was a faint hope, admittedly, barely a glimmer, but it was the first concrete idea he had had since becoming stranded. And it just might bring him the answers he needed.

Early in the twenty-first century, work would begin on a project that would eventually be known as the United Earth Space Station. There would be many delays and failures before the first module was finally placed into orbit, the date and details of which every schoolchild knew. What Quinn could not remember was when, exactly, research on the station had begun. Because one of the first pieces of technology developed in that research formed the basis of the resonator.

With that, there was a real possibility that even he, with his limited technical ability, would be able to build a frequency resonator. And it was possible that the technology he needed was under development in some laboratory right now.

If only he could find out when the research on the Earth Station project had begun.

He pondered the problem for a full day and night before the answer occurred to him.

Before the discovery of time travel, the only way of recovering information from the past had been through television and radio broadcasts of the time, randomly retrieved from outer space. Such broadcasts were still an invaluable part of their library, particularly those concerning parts of the past that had not been fully explored—like the last part of the twentieth century.

He carried those broadcasts, along with other databases essential to his mission, on microchip. All he had to do was convert them for use with the playback equipment of the day.

It was a long shot, but he had to try.

He had been at it for more than eighteen hours without a break. His head throbbed, and his throat felt raw; his muscles were stiff and sore from lack of exercise. But when he heard the sound of tires on the gravel driveway his aches faded into the background and a new and subtle energy crept through his veins. He went to the window and waited for them to come out of the garage.

Houston was wearing a pink dress with blue flowers on it, and her hair was tied back with a blue scarf. The dress was sleeveless, and the sight of her delicate bare arms wrapped around the textbooks she was carrying caused a catch in Quinn's chest. The oddest things could do that: the curve of her neck, or the way her skirt fluttered around her calves, or the sound of her laugh or the way she glanced over her shoulder without appearing to glance at all—as she did every day, as she did now—to see if he was at the window.

Quinn called down, "Mark!"

Boy and mother turned.

"Where would I find an AV cable?"

Mark grinned, and Quinn answered his own question at the same time Mark did. "Radio Shack."

Mark turned to his mother. "Can I go?"

Houston lifted an eyebrow and he corrected himself automatically. "May I? Please?"

Quinn said, "I won't keep him out long."

Houston looked up at him, shading her eyes with her hand. He wondered if her heart was beating with quick expectation, as his was. He wished he could tell her how hard he was trying for her, for them both. But even if he could have, he wouldn't. False hope was worse than no hope at all.

"Would you like to borrow the car?" she asked.

"Wouldn't you like to come along?"

She hesitated. The last time they had been closer than this window, they had been lying naked in each other's arms. He had not even joined them for meals over the past two days; not because he was avoiding her, but because he hadn't the time to spare, and anxiety had taken his appetite. He understood her hesitation. She didn't know his agenda. And he couldn't tell her.

"You really don't like to drive, do you?"

And he answered, because it was true, "We'd like the company."

She smiled. "Well, as long as you put it like that, I suppose I could pick up a few things for dinner while we're out."

"I need to be back by five, though," Mark added. "On-line conference."

Houston rolled her eyes at him. "I'll try not to interfere with your busy schedule. Just let me put my things away. I'll meet you guys at the car."

Quinn turned from the window, then caught the window frame, frowning through a wave of dizziness. He was tired. Tonight he would sleep. If he got the system hooked up this afternoon, he could afford a few hours of rest.

He went into the bathroom to splash cold water on his face, and when he returned Mark was there, examining the monitor that was linked to his hand-held unit, teaching itself to translate the computer language of this century. Quinn quickly flipped a switch, engaging a harmless entertainment program.

"Wow," Mark said. "Major multimedia. What kind of software are you running? I've never seen anything like that before."

"It's a prototype. The company sends it to me to evaluate." That was not entirely a lie. It was just that the company that had asked him to evaluate their prototype would not come into existence for another 250 years.

"Wow. Lucky." He spotted another item of interest. "Is that a videophone?"

Quinn went around the room, calmly switching off machinery. "I don't think so."

"Yeah. Who would you call?" Mark shrugged. "I mean, there's no phone up here."

Mark's eyes narrowed assessingly as he looked for the telephone link he was certain was there. He was right, too, but he would not spot the place where Quinn had tapped into the local telephone system, as it had been accomplished with a light link.

"You must be really rich," Mark murmured.

Quinn smiled. "Who's your conference with?"

"Huh?" Mark was staring at one of the computer setups, and he seemed to be thinking about something else. Then he answered, "Oh. This guy, a writer, is going to be on the science-fiction forum. You want to listen in?"

"Thanks. I have to work."

Mark looked around. "How come it's so cool up here?"

Quinn had forgotten to disengage the climate control. "It has to be, for the computers."

"Yeah, I know." A puzzled frown lingered around Mark's brow. "But it's like eighty degrees outside. And there's no air conditioning in here."

Quinn stood at the door. "Ready to go?"

Mark looked around one more time. "Yeah. Sure. You sure do have an interesting job."

Quinn forced a smile. "Yes. I do."

Houston was just coming out of the house when they came down. She had changed into jeans and a cotton T-shirt, and Quinn could not stop his eyes from tracing the curve of her hips that his hands once had cupped, the shape of her breasts that his fingers once had caressed. A spasm of longing stabbed at his chest, and it was impossible to believe they would never hold each other again like that. Impossible.

Mark climbed into the back seat and Quinn got into the passenger seat beside Houston. The silence grew awkward as she turned the car down the driveway and onto the main road.

There were a dozen things Quinn might like to have said, but with Mark listening from the back seat his choices were limited. After a time he settled on a neutral subject. "Any more trouble with the car?"

She didn't even glance at him, and her tone was too casual to be genuine. "No. It runs better than new. You must be some kind of a magician."

"I'm glad I could help."

They came to an intersection and she slowed, looking in his direction to check traffic. Her expression softened a little and she said, "Are you feeling okay? You look tired."

"I am, a little."

"You should take better care of yourself. There's a strain of flu going around."

"Yes, that's probably it. I will."

Another beat of silence. The things unspoken between them throbbed in the air. Then Houston asked, "Will you be joining us for dinner tonight?"

Too polite now. Almost stiff.

"I don't know. I'm at a critical point in my work and I'd like to see it through."

"I see."

Her voice was definitely chilly now, and he could see the tension in her arms and shoulders as she guided the car.

He said, lowering his voice a fraction, "I've been working hard lately. I hoped if I finished early I might have more time to spend . . . on other things. With friends."

"I see." Her tone was still guarded and she did not take her eyes off the road, but the tension in her arms relaxed a fraction. "That will be nice for you. Any idea how long you'll be staying yet?"

She darted a quick glance at him that revealed far more than she had probably intended—anxiety, hurt, reproach, hope. *Houston,* he thought, his throat constricting, *I am so sorry. . . .*

He answered quietly, "Not yet."

She nodded and turned her attention back to the road.

They parked in the lot of a lively little shopping strip on the outskirts of town. Houston left to do her grocery shopping, and Mark introduced Quinn to the wonders of the local Radio Shack.

Most of the equipment Quinn needed he had been able to reproduce or improvise from what he had available, so he had had very little need of the electronic supplies of the times. Now, however, his own resources were stretched to the limit, and he would have to adapt to the standards of the day.

Mark took him down the aisles, pointing out the games and gadgets that he considered cool. Then without warning, Mark said, "What's going on between you and my mom?"

Quinn was surprised, but not really shocked. Mark was an extraordinarily perceptive young boy; he had always known that.

It did not occur to him to lie. He had promised Houston he wouldn't—unless he had to. He said, "I'm not sure I know the answer to that, Mark." He could tell by the expression on Mark's face that that wasn't good enough, and he didn't blame him. He added, "I only know that your mother is the most extraordinary woman I've ever met."

Mark nodded—in approval or agreement—and replaced a video game he had been examining. "I have to take care of her, you know. I hope you're not planning to make her sad."

Quinn replied seriously, "I'll do everything in my power not to."

Mark hesitated. "My dad makes her sad a lot."

Quinn rested his hand on Mark's shoulder. "Sometimes people do that, Mark. I don't know why."

"Yeah, I know," he muttered.

Then he moved down the aisle. "The video cables are down here."

"I'm going to need a nine-pin adaptor, too."

"My teacher wants me to skip a grade next year," Mark said. "She says I'm underchallenged."

"That's good, isn't it?"

Mark shrugged. "Mom doesn't think so. She's worried about my social development."

Quinn suppressed a grin. "What do you think?"

"I think my development is fine."

Quinn let the grin break through. "I do too."

And then Mark surprised him by asking, "What would you do?"

It was a moment, Quinn knew, that called for parenting. He had no experience or training in that area and no right whatsoever to interfere.

He had never imagined he might one day be a parent. He was surprised by how natural it felt to step into the role. "Education is important. You're going to need as much as you can get to face the world you're growing up in."

Mark gave him a look that reflected a young person's impatience with equivocation. Quinn smiled. "What do you want to do, Mark?"

"I want to skip. Fifth grade is boring. And in seventh grade you can get two hours a day of computer lab. I want to skip."

Quinn said, "That's what I would have done."

"Did you skip grades when you were in school?"

"I went to a different kind of school. But once I made up my mind what I was going to do, I did what I had to do in order to accomplish my goal—sometimes at the expense of my social development."

"You turned out okay."

"That's nice of you to say, Mark."

"Don't you think so?"

Quinn smiled, but he knew the sadness was in his eyes. "Sometimes," he said, "I wish I had paid more attention to my social development."

A salesperson approached with a welcoming grin on his face. "Hello, young Mark. What can I help you with today?"

"This is my friend Quinn. He needs some stuff. Do you have the CD from the San Diego Zoo yet?"

"Got it in this morning. I loaded it up when I saw you come in. Check it out." He gestured toward a display computer and watched with a smile while Mark hurried over. He turned back to Quinn. "Nice kid. Now, what can I help you with, sir?"

Quinn told him what he needed and the salesperson bagged the items. Quinn paid with a twenty.

"Mark," he said, "let's go. Your mother will be waiting."

Reluctantly, Mark exited the program and left the computer. Quinn accepted his change, but as he went to replace his wallet in his back pocket it slipped out of his hand.

"Clumsy today," he muttered, flexing fingers that, for a moment, refused to respond. *Too many hours at the keyboard,* he thought. And he even tried to believe it.

Mark picked up his wallet but hesitated before returning it. "Hey, is this you?"

The wallet was open to the picture of Sam and him. "That's right."

"Who's the guy?"

"His name is Sam. He was a good friend of mine."

Mark studied the picture a moment longer, then seemed to remember his manners and returned the wallet. But he was quiet as they left the store, and all the way home.

HOUSTON KEPT GLANCING out the window as she prepared dinner, wondering if Quinn would join them. She had tried to be mature, had made no demands, had tried to understand. But it hurt. How could it not hurt, when the man she had made love with, the man with whom she had made herself most vulnerable and trusting, lived fifty feet away and had barely spoken to her in two days?

They had agreed, she knew. He had made her no promises, and she had promised no regrets. And in truth they had had no time to be alone; a woman with a full-time job and a young son could hardly play the femme fatale whenever the fancy struck her. Still, she had expected…something. A smile, a word, a look, something to acknowledge that they had shared the most basic and important act two people could know.

It was possible he had been working, as he had claimed, in order to spend more time with her. She wanted to believe it even though she knew the truth was that he was just trying to make the final separation easier. She did not blame him. She had known what she was doing and she was prepared to accept the consequences.

She was.

"Hey, Mom."

Houston moved guiltily away from the window and to the counter, where she sprinkled cheese over the casserole she was making for dinner. She glanced at Mark. "I thought you had some kind of computer conference. Is it over?"

"I didn't log on. Mom, what's this?"

He had a photograph album that Houston had inherited from her grandmother. It was the only link Houston had with any semblance of a "real" family, and Mark took almost as much pleasure as she did looking through the photographs that represented their heritage.

She came over to him, looking over his shoulder at the photograph he was indicating. "That's Grandpa Sam in front of the Hoover Dam," she said. "You know that. He helped build it."

But even as she spoke, her words began to dry up in her throat. Shock and a horrible, impossible certainty twisted in her stomach, lodged in her chest.

Mark asked, "Who's that with him?"

It was Quinn. It couldn't be, but...

"It must be...coincidence," she managed to say. Her voice was breathless. "Quinn...couldn't have a relative who knew Grandpa. He would have said something...."

And her head was whirling with questions. What did this mean? If there was a relationship between Quinn's family and hers, why hadn't he said something? God, she had looked at that photograph a hundred times and had never realized, had never put it together.... What could any of this mean?

Mark's face was sober, his eyes enormous behind the glasses. "Mom," he said, "Quinn has a picture just like this in his wallet. I asked him about it and he said it was a picture of him—and his friend Sam."

She stared at Mark. It was becoming harder to breathe. She said, "He was teasing you, Mark."

"I don't think so."

She couldn't even think of anything else to say. She stared at the faded black-and-white photograph, trying to think of an explanation. It was as though her mind was swathed in cotton; her thought processes were muffled, muted and indistinct.

"Mom, why would he carry a copy of this picture in his wallet? Why would he even think of a joke like that?"

With an effort, Houston drew a deep breath and squared her shoulders. "Why don't we go ask him?"

She picked up the photograph album and led the way across the lawn, up the steps to the garage apartment.

Under ordinary circumstances, it would never had occurred to her to enter a man's quarters without knocking. These were not ordinary circumstances, it was true, but perhaps she had an ulterior motive. Perhaps she wanted to see for herself what Quinn really did up there all by himself, the mysterious "work" that he couldn't explain to her or tear himself away from....

So she burst through the door, with Mark close behind, and she saw.

There was so much that the mind couldn't take it in all at once. Mark hadn't exaggerated when he said Quinn's room looked like the control center for the space shuttle. There were blinking lights and glowing panels, snaking cables and crisscrossing wires. There were computer monitors and televisions, all of them showing a different picture but only one of them including sound.

It was that one television, with picture and sound, that froze Houston in place, her attention riveted to the screen as a familiar wake-up show host said, "Good morning, America, it's Tuesday, July 2, 1996, and we're live from the Olympic Games in Atlanta, Georgia..."

Quinn stood up immediately and turned the television off, his startled expression quickly smoothing out into blankness. He stood facing Houston, his body partially hiding the equipment behind him, and said nothing.

"It's Tuesday, July 2, 1996..."

She said hoarsely, "How did you do that?"

"Good morning, America, it's Tuesday, July 2..."

"It's a tape, right?" She was trembling inside, and she didn't know why. Of course it was a tape. It had to be. "A recording."

Mark said, "How could he record something that hasn't happened yet?"

The strain of keeping her voice steady actually hurt her throat and deep into her chest. "It's some kind of trick," she insisted. "How did you do that?" *And how did you manage to have your picture taken with my grandfather sixty years ago and who are you and what are you doing here and why won't you answer me?*

Because she didn't want to hear the answers. He knew that, and so did she.

Mark said quietly, "I don't think it's a trick, Mom."

Quinn looked at Mark. For the first time he spoke, and his voice was gentle and resigned. "What do you think it is, Mark?"

"I think it's real," her son answered, with a quiet conviction that chilled Houston's soul. "I think you've come here from the future through some kind of time travel we don't know about yet, and you brought that tape with you. And I think that this isn't the first time you've come back, and that once you went all the way to 1934 and had your picture taken in front of Hoover Dam with a man named Sam. That's what I think."

Despite the apparent calmness with which Mark had reached this conclusion, he was breathing fast by the end of his speech. His eyes met Quinn's challengingly. "Am I right?"

Quinn's eyes met Houston's, and she could not believe what she saw there. She simply couldn't. Then he looked at Mark, and smiled tiredly.

"Yes, Mark," he said. "You're right."

Chapter Nine

Houston said, without expression, "That's crazy."

"I was right," Mark said. "I knew it." His voice was soft and full of wonder. "From the very first minute I knew there was something strange about you, about all this..."

And then his tone sharpened, became more animated. "That silver suit you were wearing and the helmet—some kind of time-machine gear, right?"

Quinn moved away from the computers to sit on the edge of the bed. "It's not a machine, actually. But time travel does involve a considerable change in atmospheric pressure, and the suit keeps the body functioning normally during the change."

Mark nodded enthusiastically. "Makes sense. Like deep-sea diving. If you go down too fast, you explode."

Quinn nodded. Though he spoke to Mark, his eyes were on Houston. "Something like that."

Houston didn't seem to be able to move, or think, or feel very much at all. She stood there frozen in the doorway, staring at this man she thought she knew, this man she might even have *loved,* and it was all she could do to keep breathing.

She said hoarsely, "Stop it. Stop telling lies to my son."

She saw the hurt cross Quinn's face, though it barely registered with her. But she heard Mark say, "He's not lying, Mom. Don't you see it all makes sense? This explains everything! The only thing I can't figure out is..." A small frown creased his brow. "Why now, why us? Unless..."

Mark's eyes grew round with excitement. "Something's going to happen, isn't it? To me, or Mom, or someone we know—something that changes history, and you're here to stop it!"

Quinn smiled faintly. He seemed relaxed now, relieved to have it all out in the open. "Only in books and movies, Mark. The truth is, we've found that it's impossible to interfere in any measurable way with history—it's a very complicated theory that you will actually study in college physics, but that won't be proven for a couple of hundred years."

Mark obviously didn't like that. "But then why time travel at all? When we first met you, you said you had a project—so what is it?"

"I already told you. I'm a field historian, and my mission is to observe and record what life was really like in the twentieth century."

"That's all?" He seemed disappointed.

"In my century, history is the most valuable thing we learn, and historians are heroes. To contribute in some way to the reconstruction of our past is the most important mission a man can undertake."

Mark's tone was still skeptical. "Yeah, but how much can you learn in a place like Carsonville?"

Quinn's answer was wry. "The truth is, I didn't intend to land in Carsonville—or your apple tree, for that matter. There was a malfunction in my equipment. I was supposed to be in Chicago in 1984."

Mark said softly, "Man." Then, "And so how did you end up at Hoover Dam in 1934?"

"The building of the dam was a history-making event, and I was there to record it—or as much of it as I could. I actually worked on the dam for several months..." And then he stopped, and inquired curiously, "How did you know about that, anyway?"

"That picture you have," Mark explained, "the one of you and Sam. We have one just like it. Sam was my great-grandfather."

Quinn stood up slowly, shock draining through his face. "What?"

"Sure." Mark turned to Houston, who was still clutching the photograph album. "Show him, Mom."

Mark reached for the album, but Houston grabbed his arm, pulling him close to her in a protective gesture, then shoving him behind her. "Get out of here, Mark," she said, breathing hard.

"But—"

"Mark, I mean it! Get out of here!" Her voice had taken on the high thin edge of hysteria, and she knew it but she didn't care. It frightened Mark enough to obey her without question, and that was all that mattered.

Mark moved away from her, hesitantly at first, and then she heard his footsteps moving down the stairs. She took a backward step toward the door, holding the photograph album tight against her chest like a shield. She looked at Quinn, and she felt such a wave of horror and revulsion that she could hardly catch her breath to speak.

"I want you out of here." Her voice was quavering. She was shaking. "Today. You and all this—" she made a small tight gesture toward the equipment that surrounded them "—junk." *"It's Tuesday, July 2, 1996."* "Don't ever bother me or my son, again. You're a crazy person. You lied. I want you out."

The hurt that crossed his face tore at her heart. Even as it terrified her.

"I'm not lying, Houston," he said. "I promised you I wouldn't lie unless I had to and I haven't. I'm tired of the secrets. There's no point, anyway. Accuse me of anything else but not of lying."

He took a small, entreating step toward her, and that was more than she could bear. The photograph album slipped from her hands as she turned, with a small cry, for the door. Quinn called after her, but she plunged recklessly down the stairs and did not look back.

HOUSTON WAS vaguely aware of Mark as she rushed across the lawn, but she sent him to the house with a harsh order. She didn't know where she was going or why; she only knew that she had to get away—from this place, from Mark, from Quinn, from the insanity. So she walked blindly and she kept on walking, across the drive, down the slope, over the meadow, until she found herself at the apple tree. There she leaned her cheek against the cool smooth bark and shook with sobs of frustration and confusion.

This couldn't be happening to her, not again. She couldn't have chosen the wrong man again; she couldn't have been taken in by another con artist. She was the sensible one, the careful one; she had done one impulsive, reckless thing in her whole life and look what it had gotten her. A raving lunatic, a certifiable madman.... She had tried so hard to build a safe, secure world for Mark, to give him the sane, orderly home life she had never had. Things like this didn't happen to her. She *guarded* against things like this.

And she had failed.

She didn't hear him come up behind her, but she felt the weight of his hand on her shoulder. She jerked away violently and spun around to confront him.

"Go away!" she cried hoarsely. As hard as she tried to prevent it, the hot tears spilled over, tears of anger and fear, sorrow and disappointment. "Stay away from me, I mean it! Just stay away."

"Houston." His eyes were dark with pain, and he half-lifted one hand in entreaty. "I'm not lying to you, I swear it. You've stood beside me through so much. You've given me so many chances. Don't give up on me now! I wanted to tell you—I didn't even realize how much I wanted to tell you until now. And by telling you the truth I've broken the last and most important rule of my time, but it *is* the truth. By all that you call holy, Houston, you have to believe me. It is the truth.

"Don't you think I know that?" she cried.

The horror of her own words and the certainty behind them swirled around her and threatened to overwhelm her. She pressed her fingers into her hot, wet face as though to blot them out. She sensed, rather than saw, Quinn take a step toward her, but she staggered back, crying, "No! Just leave me alone!"

He said quietly, "I can't do that, Houston. If I could do that, none of this would have happened."

Houston dragged in one last sobbing breath and abruptly squared her shoulders, scrubbing away tears with the palms of her hands. Bracing her hands against the trunk of the tree behind her, she faced him. She said, as steadily as she could, "I don't need this. I can't deal with this. I don't want to know any of this.''

"I'm sorry."

She gulped in another wet breath, dashed away another handful of tears. "I have a son to raise. He's not going to grow up with leprechauns and crystal balls and magic castles and...and spacemen! He's not going to grow up thinking a magic wand can make dreams come true or that a man who falls out of an apple tree can tell the future. Do you understand that? I want better than that for him, for us! I've spent my life trying to make sure he had better.... Oh, God, why did you have to pick us?''

And with that all the strength seemed to leave her and all the need for it. With her back against the tree trunk she sank to the ground and buried her face in her updrawn knees.

Quinn sat beside her and drew her into his arms, holding her, gently rocking back and forth. "I know," he whispered. "I'm sorry. I know."

"I hate you for this," she sobbed. "Why did you have to do this, why?"

And he just said, "I know."

And he held her until, a long time later, weary with crying and too numb to think anymore, she pushed him away.

She ran a shaking hand over her face, pushing back her damp hair. She took a couple of deep breaths. Twilight was falling, lending its soft romantic glow to the countryside around them. Beneath the low-hanging branches of the apple tree the shadows were even deeper, sealing her in with him, separate from the world. Yet the world went on as usual, just beyond the tree, just outside her reach.

She said, without much expression at all, "I can't deal with this now, Quinn. I have to get back to the house. Mark will be worried. I can't deal with this."

He said quietly, "I don't know how to get back, Houston."

She turned slowly and looked at him. She saw the same face that had caused her breath to catch in her throat more than once. The same scarred eyebrow, the same firm chin, the same hazel eyes. The crisp sandy hair, the gentle lines around his eyes, the same firm mouth...a little sadder now, a little more tired. But it was the face she had wanted to love, had not been able to stop herself from loving...

"That's how it all started," he continued. "I'm here by accident—and I can't get back. I never meant to hurt you."

Houston swallowed hard, giving a little shake of her head as though to ground herself in reality. "I have to go," she said. Somehow she managed to get to her feet. "I have to make dinner."

He stood, too, but he said nothing.

She walked toward the house on legs that were only slightly wobbly. She had only gone a few steps before she stopped. She did not turn around. "Come by. After dinner. We'll talk."

SHE SAT on one of the rocking chairs on the front porch, listening to the crickets and the night birds, rocking back and forth. The glow from the house illuminated the porch, but the driveway and yard were in shadows. Occasionally she could hear the whoosh of tires from the highway and see the flash of headlights. Except for that she could have been all alone on an alien planet.

Lost. Stranded.

She kept thinking back over everything that had happened since she had met Quinn, all the clues she had missed, all the questions she had never asked. Her ten-year-old son had known something was wrong, but she hadn't.

Maybe she hadn't asked the questions because somewhere deep inside she had known she would not be able to accept the answers.

He had told her he was stranded. He had told her he was a field historian. He had told her his job involved studying and recording human events. Everything else she had made up, a deliberate smoke screen to satisfy her questing mind before it asked a question he could not answer. Never once had she asked about the shiny suit. All those televisions, his extraordinary interest in current events, his extraordinary ignorance about certain common, everyday things—the clues had been there. Quinn had not made a deliberate effort to conceal anything from her. How could she be angry with him? His only crime had been to come into her life at all, to say yes when she invited him to stay.

"Mom?"

Mark's voice, small and uncertain, drew her out of her musings. He stood in the doorway, behind the screen, reluctant to come out.

He said, "I put the leftovers away and cleaned up the kitchen."

Houston did not remember eating dinner. She hoped Mark had.

"Thanks, sweetheart."

She extended her hand for him, and he came outside. She put her arm around him and drew him close. "Are you too big to sit on my lap?"

"Yeah," he admitted. "But I will this once if you won't tell anybody."

"I promise."

He sat on her knee and she hugged him. "I love you, Mark."

"Love you, too, Mom."

She took comfort in her son's embrace, in the peace of the night, in the shared moment. Then Mark asked, "Why are you mad?"

Houston leaned back, and Mark wriggled forward on her knee so that he could see her face. Houston sighed. "I'm not mad, Mark. It's complicated, but . . . I'm not mad."

"You acted like it. You were yelling at Quinn."

"I know."

"It's not like he can help it, you know."

She tried to smile. "You're right about that."

Mark was thoughtful for a moment, then said, "Whatever he did to make you upset, I don't think he meant it."

"Whatever he did..." Only to a ten-year-old would a man's announcement that he had traveled back in time from a future neither of them understood be considered *"whatever he did."* She patted Mark on the back. "I'm sure he didn't. The problem is with me, not Quinn." And she wished she could be a ten-year-old, to see and know and accept with the unquestioning faith of a child.

Mark said, "I mean, Mom, you've got to see how neat this is. You know how they're always talking in Sunday school about miracles—well, *this* is what I call a miracle."

Houston disagreed gently. "Miracles are generally considered a gift from God."

"A man who hasn't even been born yet falls out of your apple tree, out of all the apple trees in the world? That's not a gift from God?"

A man overcame the laws of space and time to make her believe she could love again.... That wasn't a miracle? Houston didn't know what to say.

"All I know is, this is better than any of the stories they tell in Sunday school," Mark said.

Houston started to agree, however absently, then was struck by a pang of alarm. "Mark, you know you can't tell anyone about this, don't you?"

He gave her an *aw, Mom* look. "Of course I do. Do you think I want G-men in environmental suits crawling all over the place, trying to drag Quinn back to their lab?"

Houston suppressed a smile. "Of course not."

"But," Mark insisted, "think about it. All the things he knows, all he could tell us. Like what's going to happen to the stock market and what I'm going to be when I grow up and if you're ever going to get married again—"

"I'm afraid it doesn't work that way, Mark."

Quinn's voice came quietly out of the darkness, startling them both. He was standing at the bottom of the steps, and as Mark scrambled out of his mother's lap Quinn climbed up to them, the photograph album in his hand.

"I thought I'd better return this," Quinn said, handing it to Houston. "You dropped it earlier."

Houston took the photograph album, her heart speeding at the sight of him, at the sound of his voice. Was it from dread or anxiety, wonder or fear—or the sheer instinctual thrill of having him near? Her mind might know a dozen rational reasons to push him away, but her body had not heard the news yet.

Mark hoisted himself onto the porch rail. "How does it work?" he asked.

Quinn was looking at Houston, uncertain of his welcome. Houston invited in a subdued tone, "Sit down, Quinn."

Quinn took the rocking chair on the opposite side of the doorway, a good eight feet away from her. Houston relaxed.

Quinn said, "Think about that, Mark. There's no way for me to know the details of individuals' lives. Do you know who Aristotle's next-door neighbor was, and what he grew up to be?"

Mark was obviously unsure who Aristotle was, and Houston did not enlighten him. It would give him something to look up in his encyclopedia later—which, knowing Mark, he would be sure to do.

"Well, I guess not," Mark said. "But things like who won the Superbowl and who's going to win the election . . ."

Quinn shook his head. "Those are the kinds of things I'm here to find out."

As hard as she tried to close herself off to this incredible conversation, as much as she wanted to pretend it wasn't happening, Houston was intrigued. If Mark had not asked the next question, she would have.

"What do you mean? Don't you guys have history books?"

Quinn shook his head. "A great deal of our history has been lost, and even greater parts have been rewritten. Don't look so surprised—it happened in your time, too. History has always been a temporary thing, depending on who was in power—until time travel, that is. Now for the first time we're able to find out what really happened."

"Yeah, but that doesn't make sense. You had that tape—or whatever it was—about the Olympics. It looked just like a real news show, but it hasn't happened yet. So you've got to have some kind of—I don't know, machine or something—that records the future."

Quinn smiled. "Good theory, Mark. But if you think about it for a minute I think you'll discover a much simpler explanation. What is one of the first things we learn about energy?"

He's good, Houston thought. And she felt a rush of affection for him that took her by surprise.

"That it can't be created or destroyed," Mark said.

"That it never goes away," added Houston softly.

Quinn cast her an approving glance. He said to Mark, "And what is the essence of television and radio waves?"

"Energy. Oh, man," Mark said, understanding. "That's right. Every time something is broadcast for television, it just goes on into outer space and floats around out there as light energy forever."

"That's right," Quinn said, and Houston felt a surge of pride in her son. "Sometimes we're able to retrieve those light waves and reconstruct them into their original broadcasts, but it's a difficult and time-consuming task—and not very reliable. If you know the laws of probability, you could calculate the odds of one particular light beam striking one of our retrieval satellites at just the right moment. If we had a way to control or track the transmissions, it would be a different matter. As it is, we have to just take our chances. We've been collecting transmissions for about a hundred years now, and we have only a handful of usable tapes.''

Mark was silent, digesting this.

After a moment, he said, ''What I don't understand is, how could anybody lose history? What happened?''

Quinn hesitated, and Houston tensed. Then he said, ''There are some things you don't need to know, Mark, and it would be wrong of me to tell you. Can you accept that?''

Mark gave it a moment's thought. ''Sure. Cool.''

Then he said, ''So what year are you from, anyway?''

Quinn glanced at Houston, and she thought he might decline to answer out of consideration for her. The resilience of the young was a wonderful thing, and it was obvious Mark was adjusting to the new influx of information with far more ease than was Houston. She braced herself for the answer.

''When I left,'' Quinn said, ''the year was 2318.''

Houston felt a peculiar wave of light-headedness drain through her, as though *she* had made the trip back in time—all in the space between one breath and another.

''Wow,'' Mark said. ''Captain's log, star date.''

Three hundred years. Her grandchildren, and her grandchildren's grandchildren, would be long gone by then. Quinn did not belong here, and she could not even imagine the place he did belong. Mark had put it best: Quinn hadn't even been born yet. Strictly speaking, he didn't even exist.

As far as star-crossed lovers went, one could hardly surpass that.

"So if it's not a time machine," Mark asked, "how *do* you do it?"

Houston said uncertainly, "Mark, I don't think you should pester Quinn with all these questions."

"No." Quinn glanced at her quickly. "I'd like to answer if you don't mind. I feel I owe you both an explanation, or at least as much of one as I can give."

Houston felt like an intruder between the two of them, but she had to admit she was curious. Even though she knew she wouldn't understand it, she wanted to hear the answer.

Quinn chose his words carefully. "I can't give you details, Mark, mostly because my reference words haven't come into use in your language yet. But basically what we discovered is that by manipulating the magnetic fields that surround the human body we can alter the time-space continuum enough to actually move that body through time."

"So what you're saying," Mark interrupted eagerly, "is that time is an absolute. Static."

Quinn nodded. "More or less."

"Man! Nobody's thinking that now! I mean, all the science-fiction guys are into the infinite-possibilities, alternate-realities hypothesis."

Houston stared at her son. She felt, in addition to everything else, as though she were the fifth grader and he were the teacher.

"Don't fall into the trap of thinking it's as simple as I make it sound," Quinn warned. "There are volumes of exceptions and variables involved."

"Sure. Naturally. So in the twenty-fourth century people can just pop back and forth in time whenever they want?"

"Wait a minute." Houston had tried to keep herself aloof, separate from the conversation and all it implied, hoping that by doing so, she could hold on to the fragile scraps of her world as she knew it. But she couldn't stay silent any longer. She pressed two fingers to her temple, marshaling her thoughts, and she said, "This is where I get off. I mean—some of it, sure. But if you're telling me people from the twenty-fourth century are wandering around among us like...like vacationers at Club Med...no. That I won't buy. I mean, we would have noticed. There would be signs—"

"Mom," explained Mark patiently, "there *are*. Batteries found in the pyramids. Three-thousand-year-old skulls with brain-surgery scars on them. Where would those things have come from if not the future?"

"My... goodness." The words were drawn from her slowly as another wave of altered reality hit her. This was happening. This was real.

She turned to Quinn, questioning, almost hoping he would deny it. But he didn't.

"One of our most important rules is that we not interfere with the normal course of events, and leave nothing behind," he said. "But mistakes were made before we had the rules, and sometimes accidents happen... like the one that happened to me."

"What?" Mark insisted. "What happened?"

"Time travel makes use of a device called a frequency resonator," Quinn said. "It aligns the magnetic fields around the body and converts them into readable energy, then resonates—or transfers—the signal to an amplifier, which of course is located in the twenty-fourth century. Many things can disturb the resonator field, though, particularly when you're traveling into time periods with some technological sophistication—which is one of the things that makes the last half of the twentieth century the most dangerous, and least explored, period of history."

Yet he was here, Houston thought. He had chosen the most dangerous assignment, the one most desperately needed, the one no one else would take. But hadn't she sensed that about him from the first? The reckless adventurer, intrepid explorer... She simply had never before thought of the streets of her own small town as a jungle to be mapped.

"We use safeguards, of course," Quinn was saying, "but they don't always work. Some kind of system failure put me ten years and several hundred miles off course, but that wasn't the worst problem. During the fall from your tree a lot of my equipment was broken and one very important piece was lost."

"The resonator?" Mark asked.

Quinn nodded.

"But how can you get back without it?"

He answered, "I can't."

"Wow. Then you're stuck here? You just have to stay, and live like a twentieth-century man, forever?"

Quinn didn't answer right away. Perhaps it was that silence that alerted Houston, perhaps it was some kind of sixth sense, but she knew something was wrong. She strained to see his face, but he sat in the shadows and his expression was unreadable.

"I can't stay, Mark." He seemed to be choosing his words carefully. "Every time you travel back in time, it's like a stopwatch is set. You have a certain number of days to complete your assignment and return. My time is almost up. I have to go back."

Houston did not understand the heaviness in her chest, the hollowness in her stomach. He had told her from the beginning that he would leave her. He had never pretended permanence. He wasn't even *real*; she had established that in her mind already. She didn't want him to be real. She had been furious and betrayed to learn he had deceived her in the first place. Why should she feel so hurt to learn he was leaving?

She was so wrapped up in her own shock and misery that she didn't even notice her son's prolonged silence until he spoke. His tone was subdued. "So. I guess you have to find that resonator thing, huh?"

Just when she thought her poor battered heart could not take any more, she felt a new fissure rend it for Mark's sake. First his father, now Quinn. Every man he had ever trusted had betrayed him in the end. And Quinn was more than a friend. In the few weeks he had been here, he had been more of a father to Mark than Mike ever had.

And more of a husband to Houston.

"I've looked everywhere," Quinn said. "It's likely it was lost in transit. I'm going to have to try to build one."

"Can you do that?"

"I don't know," Quinn admitted. "Not without help. I was hoping maybe you could help me."

"Yeah . . . well, maybe."

The forced nonchalance in Mark's tone disguised his pride and excitement at being asked. Once again Quinn had known exactly the right thing to say, and once again mother and son responded to it. How could she hate him? How could she be sorry for what he had brought into their lives, however temporary it might have been? How could she be angry with him? He had never promised them more.

Mark said, "Of course you'd have to tell me what you're looking for."

There followed a technical discussion that seemed somehow involved with subatomic physics and that, since it included very few principles relevant to third graders, left Houston completely lost. Mark seemed to follow him, though—or if he did not, at least he gave the appearance of doing so.

"Do you know what?" Mark said after he was finished. "This may sound crazy but..."

He shared a shy grin with Quinn, both of them realizing that nothing Mark could say would sound as crazy as what Quinn had just asked them both to believe.

"You remember that science-fiction forum I told you about?" Mark went on. "Well, I was thinking. It's not just regular guys on there, but some big-name writers, too. A lot of them are scientists."

"And if anyone would have access to the latest technological information," Quinn said, following his thought, "they would."

Mark nodded enthusiastically. "Not only that, but these guys make their living imagining things—building things like your resonator in their heads. What you don't know, I bet they could figure out."

"Mark, that's a wonderful idea." Quinn's voice was rich with relief.

"Maybe if we pretended we were writing a book—"

"Of course."

"No one would have to know it was for real."

"It's worth a chance."

Mark jumped down from the rail. "I'm going to go up and start nosing around right now. You want to come?"

Quinn said, "Let me write down what I remember about the construction. There's no point in opening a dialogue until we have some concrete questions to ask."

"Right. I'll just go and get some contacts lined up."

Mark dashed past Houston into the house, and she half lifted a hand as though to stop him but let it fall again. She felt as though she should say something about bedtime and school tomorrow, but such concerns seemed mundane in the extreme under the circumstances. Nothing about this situation was normal, and pretending otherwise would not make it so.

So she let him go.

Chapter Ten

When Mark was gone she stole a glance at Quinn through the shadows. The silence between them felt awkward. To break it, she said, "He amazes me sometimes. Most of the time, in fact. Are you sure you can't tell me anything about his future?"

She hated the way that sounded. She hated the way that made her feel. Only days ago she had lain naked with him, arms and legs entwined, sharing secrets and making wishes the way lovers did. Now she was addressing him as though he were omnipotent, a seer, a god. She was embarrassed. So was he.

"No. Sorry. Sometimes the most frustrating thing about my work is not knowing things like that—or even more important things."

"Of course," she murmured uncomfortably. "I didn't mean to imply...I mean, in the whole scheme of history the fate of one small boy doesn't seem very important, does it?"

He smiled across the porch at her. "It depends on the boy, I suspect. And I have a feeling Mark will make his fair contribution to history."

She tried to return his smile, but it faded into awkwardness. Given his vast perspective on the state of the world, given his adventures in this and other centuries, given his easy knowledge of things her twentieth-century mind could not even comprehend were they explained to her—anything Houston said sounded stupid to her own ears. She had a thousand questions she was suddenly too shy to ask, for the man she once had known and thought she could love was now a stranger.

Heloise the cat trotted up the steps from the yard, looking sleek and satisfied after her twilight prowl, and went straight to Quinn. Apparently she had missed the news and did not know that her friend's status in the family had changed. She walked right over to him, arched her back and meowed.

Quinn extended his hand and murmured absently, "Yes, I think you're right."

The cat rubbed its head and back against Quinn's hand with a musical half-purr, half-mew that made Quinn smile. "You are indeed a fascinating creature."

Houston stared at him. "What *is* it with you and that cat?"

He glanced at her, a spark of his old easy amusement in the curve of his mouth. "In my time," he said, "cats are a rare and valuable species. You have to be on a waiting list for years before even being interviewed to be matched with one."

A nervous laugh escaped Houston. "You're kidding me, right? I mean, granted, a lot can happen in three hundred years but . . ." And she peered at him closely through the darkness. "You talk to that cat as though—well, as though she talks back. You don't mean to tell me . . . ?"

She left the speculation unspoken and he laughed softly. "That cats are going to develop the ability to speak over the next three centuries? No."

Houston relaxed, then he added, "However, we will discover some interesting things about the value of learning to communicate with other species."

Houston opened her mouth to question, then shook her head. "No. I don't want to know."

She thought, in the dark, she could see the faintest hint of a twinkle in his eye. "Perhaps that's best."

The twist of conversation had eased some of the tension between them, and Quinn's tone sounded a little more relaxed as he said, "Look. The moon's coming up." He looked across the porch at her. "Would you walk with me a little?"

Houston hesitated, then stood up. They walked down the steps together, and moved across the moonlit lawn. It was a moment before either of them spoke, and when they did it was at the same time.

"Listen, it's just that—"

"I wanted to tell you—"

They stopped, and turned to look at each other. Quinn said, "Go ahead."

And Houston insisted, "No, please—you."

They started to walk again. Quinn's voice was quiet against the background of gently chirping crickets; they might have been discussing sports or politics or simple domestic matters, anything except what they were discussing.

He said, "I've always been kind of a—you have a good word for it—hotshot, I think it is. Don't get me wrong, it takes a certain amount of recklessness and independence to do what I do, and the profession has always attracted the adventurous type. But—I don't know. I've been accused of being a loose cannon. Maybe they were right. I've just always done things my own way, and this time, everything I've done has been wrong. I should never have stayed here. There are procedures that cover this sort of thing, and I didn't follow them. Once I stayed, I never should have gotten as involved as I did with you and Mark. I interfered in your lives. I...the most important rule I broke was in allowing myself to care for you... to make love with you. That was wrong. I knew I couldn't stay. I knew my leaving would hurt you. And I knew it was wrong. Houston, I'm sorry."

She drew a breath and released it a little more shakily than she had intended. She wanted to be mature about this. She did.

"I just feel like such an idiot, that's all. All that nonsense about destiny, about you seeming so familiar to me—of course you did, I must have seen that picture of you and Grandpa Sam a dozen times. I mean, I know you couldn't tell me—I wouldn't have believed it anyway—but I just wish I'd known before I made a complete fool of myself.''

He made a move as though to touch her arm, but she sidestepped him—casually, she hoped.

''You didn't make a fool of yourself,'' he told her.

''So.'' The effort she made to keep her tone easy made it sound too bright, almost brittle. ''What is it—do you guys get assigned a family or something, to follow our progress down through the centuries, like migratory birds?''

''What?''

''Because I've got to tell you, I don't much like feeling like a laboratory animal, and if that's an example of the kind of progress we make in three hundred years—''

''Houston, what are you talking about?''

''My grandfather, then me,'' she explained impatiently. Her nerves were starting to feel a little raw; it might have had something to do with the tears that were stinging her eyes. ''I guess you were around for my parents, too—that must have been interesting! And all that stuff I was telling you about them—''

''Houston, I don't know your parents.''

''I just hate it that it was all so...planned! So phony and manipulative. God knows I'm not big on romance, but there are some illusions even I like to keep. I mean, I *know* there's no such thing as destiny, but I'd like to at least believe in spontaneity.''

"I didn't know he was your grandfather," Quinn said quietly.

Houston stopped, and turned to him. "What?"

"He was my friend. I left him in 1934, and except to find out the date and manner of his death, I never knew anything more about him. I had no idea he had children. I certainly never expected to meet one of his descendants—and fall in love with her.''

Fall in love. He had said that. She didn't want to hear that. It made no difference now; it meant nothing. But he had said it and she had heard it and there was a tightening inside her, a leaping for joy, a yearning toward him. *Love.* Yes.

With every ounce of will she had, she pushed the tumbling emotions down. Yet she couldn't stop herself from searching his eyes in the moonlight, trying to find...something. Hope, truth, promise... something.

"I don't understand. If you didn't know it was my grandfather, if you didn't do it on purpose, then how...?''

He pushed his fingers through his hair and shook his head. "I don't know. I've been thinking about it all afternoon. The odds against that happening, out of all the hundreds of millions of people who have lived since I left Sam, that a technical malfunction, an accident, should put me in the front yard of his granddaughter...''

"Maybe they're connected," she suggested. "The accident that brought you here and your time with my grandfather. Maybe that machine of yours has some kind of trace memory...."

Quinn looked at her soberly. "Maybe," he said, "it was destiny."

He was standing close, but he didn't touch her; he didn't have to. His warmth caressed her, and the tenderness in his eyes drew her into his embrace. She thought helplessly, *I never asked for this...I don't want this...I can't love you. I can't.*

If only she could convince her heart of that.

"When I chose to go into this work," Quinn said softly, "I knew I would never have a family of my own. It was my decision, the price I paid for the life I lead. I've never regretted it—until I came here. You and Mark let me borrow your lives for a time, showed me what I might have had if I had chosen differently, and you even let me pretend it was mine. Houston," he said earnestly, his voice hoarsening with emotion, "if I could stay with you I would. I know you probably don't want me to anymore—"

A protest formed in her throat but emerged only as a stifled moan of denial.

"But I want you to know I've done my best. I wouldn't have had this happen to you for all the world."

Houston knew she should step away, turn back toward the house, pretend the last few moments of this conversation had never happened. She couldn't love him. She couldn't have him in her life. This couldn't be happening to her.

But she couldn't move away from him. She couldn't even stop looking at him. "Why—why can't you stay?" Her heart was beating slow and hard. Maybe he would stay, if she asked. *Please stay...*

He dropped his eyes. She felt the whisper of his breath across her cheek. "I didn't want to tell Mark," he said quietly. "I thought you should decide how much he should know."

Something cold and clammy coiled in her stomach. It was a sensation she had grown familiar with over the course of the day: dread.

Quinn started walking again, his shoulder brushing hers. He didn't look at her now, and his tone was detached, almost clinical. "One of the first problems we encountered in the early days of time travel was the fact that our bodies simply weren't accustomed to the conditions of earth in the past, and we therefore had no natural immunity to even the most common bacteria and viruses you encounter every day. The same, of course, would be true if you were to transport back to the Middle Ages—you would die of food poisoning with your first meal, if the water or airborne bacteria didn't get you first. We aren't born with tolerances for diseases, you know. We have to develop immunity through exposure. And when a man is careering through time, he has no chance to develop a natural resistance to the infections of any one time period."

Houston listened carefully, her heart pounding in her chest.

"We finally developed a serum that would bolster our immune systems so that we could resist the toxins and diseases of the distant past. Unfortunately, after a certain amount of time—twenty-three days, to be exact—the serum itself becomes toxic to us. So when we travel back in time, we carry with us only twenty-three doses of the serum."

Houston's throat felt so tight that she could barely speak. "But you've already been here almost a month."

Quinn nodded. "When I realized it wasn't likely that I would be able to get back before the serum ran out, I started cutting the doses in half. But even that won't last much longer."

He stopped and looked down at her gravely. "So you see, it's not really my choice. One way or another—I can't stay."

There was a strange twisting low in Houston's chest, like a heart being torn in two. She said with an effort, "How long?"

And he answered, "About ten days."

Her breath died away, and for a moment she couldn't speak. For a moment there seemed no point—in speaking, thinking, breathing, caring. Even the night was still, crickets having sung their last, the breeze having dried up at its source. That was how she felt. Dried up at the source.

But she knew it wasn't that easy. Nothing would ever be that easy, or that painless. And she had a feeling that for her—for them—the pain had only begun.

She made herself look up at him. She tried to smile. "Then," she said, simply, and with all the courage she possessed, "we'll just have to find a way to get you home, won't we?"

Chapter Eleven

Every year the last day of school was celebrated with an informal skating party hosted by the class mothers while Millie invited her staff to a "thanks for a job well done" pool party at her home. This year neither Mark nor Houston was interested in attending.

"Hot date?" Millie teased her with a wink. "When am I going to meet this superhunk, anyway?"

Houston replied distractedly, "Actually, I was hoping to get to the library at the university before it closed."

Millie widened her eyes. "Library? University? Hello? School's out—or did you think all this paper in the halls was from a ticker-tape parade?"

Typical of last-day-of-school students everywhere, they had emptied their notebooks and their lockers in a random pattern of destruction. It was the philosophy of the administration—who admittedly grew a little lax this time of the year—that if this was the worst they had to tolerate in the way of vandalism, they were ahead of the game.

Houston tried to look interested in the conversation—and in her friend, as they walked out of the building together. "I have a kind of special project I'm working on. Nothing to do with school."

The last few days of school had been torment for her. She felt as though she were living in two different worlds: the one was filled with restless third-graders who depended on her to make certain they grew into responsible, reasonably well-educated citizens, and that demanded her full attention. The other revolved around a man who was not even supposed to exist outside science-fiction novels and who depended on her for his very life, and that demanded her full attention. Had she been required to play both roles for another single day, she was sure she would have been torn in two.

Millie said, "Something exciting, I hope."

"Hmm?" Houston caught herself and added quickly, "Oh, yes. Very." If only she knew.

But Millie looked concerned and Houston could sense more questions coming. So she swooped forward to brush her friend's cheek with a kiss. "Thanks for a great year, Millie. Have fun at the party without me. I'll call you in a few days."

She hurried out to her car, where Mark was already waiting. Immediately, he asked, "Are you sure you don't need me to go with you to the university, Mom?"

"Thanks, but you and Quinn need to be working on the computer. Quinn gave me a list of books."

"Yeah, but you really don't know much about the topic. I might spot things you can't."

"I'll just photocopy everything."

Mark was thoughtful as she started the car. She had been letting him stay up too late and he looked tired. She felt a stab of motherly guilt for that, but what kind of mother would she be if she had taught her son that regular bedtime was more important than a man's life?

She had told Mark the truth about Quinn's deadline because she felt he deserved to know, and Mark had taken it far better than she had. He seemed relieved to know that Quinn was not leaving because he wanted to. And by involving him in the solution to the problem, Quinn had given him some sense of control over the situation.

Houston only hoped he did not feel responsible if he failed.

He said now, "Quinn said you can't take things that belong in the past through the time-travel channel into the future."

Houston glanced at him. "Why would you want to?"

"We were just talking about it the other night— artifacts and things, you know, for museums. And he said it couldn't be done. And that the only things you could bring with you into the past had to fit on your tool belt or in your helmet, and that they were locked into the same frequency you were when you were transported through."

Houston knew he was not merely engaging in idle speculation, but she couldn't quite follow what he was getting at. She said carefully, "Yes?"

"So I was thinking . . . with all those safeguards, I just don't think it's very likely that the most important thing you have, the one piece of equipment that would take you back where you belong, could just disappear in transit. It has to have come through with Quinn. He must have lost it somewhere around the apple tree. He *must* have."

"But he looked. We've been all through that. He said he spent almost a whole week looking."

"Then he must have missed it. We'll have to look again."

Suddenly Houston understood. She felt a hollowness in the pit of her stomach. "It's not going well, is it?"

Mark shook his head slowly. "I don't think so. Quinn won't say anything . . . but I don't think so."

Houston reached across the seat and squeezed his knee, but she had no other comfort to offer.

IT WAS AFTER DARK when Houston returned home. She went first to check on Mark and found him stretched out on his bed with a pen and notebook beside him, fully dressed and sound asleep. The computer was on, but the starfield screen blanker was in place, indicating it had been some time since anyone had used the keyboard or mouse. Houston didn't risk waking Mark by taking off his shoes or even his glasses but covered him with a blanket and left the room, leaving the computer untouched.

In the kitchen, crumbs on the counter and dishes in the sink told her someone had made dinner— sandwiches, from the looks of it—and again she felt a prickle of guilt. But she had very little time or energy to waste on counter-productive emotions. She drank a glass of milk, then gathered up the books she had gotten from the library and crossed the lawn to Quinn's apartment.

The outdoor lights that illuminated the stairs were on, and Houston didn't realize until she reached the top step, that the lights from the window were more subdued than usual. She knocked softly. When there was no answer, she opened the door.

"Quinn?"

The room was lighted only by the glow of computer screens and the rows of odd little colored lights that represented some kind of electronic circuitry. The effect was a soft yellow illumination with shadows of red and green reflected off the ceiling. The bed was partially in shadow, but she could make out Quinn's form on it. She was glad. He, too, had been working night and day, and she worried about him.

She looked for a place to put the books, found a clear corner on one of the computer tables and turned to leave as quietly as she had come.

"I'm awake," Quinn said.

She turned toward him. "I didn't mean to disturb you."

"You didn't." The springs creaked as he sat up, propping his shoulders against the wall. "I had a headache, thought I'd rest my eyes."

"Would you like me to get something for it?"

"No, it's gone now." And he smiled. "I think it went away when I saw you."

There was something warm and intimate about the gentle lighting, voices coming to each other through the semidarkness, faces sensed but not entirely seen. Barriers were lowered somehow; words seemed easier. After a moment's hesitation, she crossed the room toward him, stepping carefully over cables and skirting stacks of books and cartons of periodicals.

She sat on the edge of the bed. "I wasn't able to find some of the titles. I placed an inter-library loan request, but it may take a few days."

Quinn nodded. "We have a few days."

He was wearing jeans and a long-sleeved shirt that was open over his bare chest. His hair was rumpled and his feet were bare. Even in the uncertain light she could see the fatigue that lined his face, and she wanted to lay her hand against that face, to comfort him.

"I've never seen you shave."

If he was surprised by the non sequitur, he didn't show it. "In my time, facial hair is considered unsanitary and unattractive. Most men have their beards permanently removed through a simple cosmetic procedure." He paused, and she saw the corner of a smile lurked around his lips. "The same procedure is used to remove hair from their heads."

Houston lifted her eyebrows. "Why would anyone want to do that?"

"Because it's the fashion."

"Baldness?"

He nodded, eyes twinkling. "Sleek and sexy, I believe is the phrase."

She stared at him for a moment, straining to discern more of his expression in the low light, then struck him playfully on the leg.

"You're teasing me! Why am I so gullible?"

"It's the truth," he insisted, catching her hand. "I keep my hair because I don't want to be conspicuous in this time period, but in my time period I'm very conspicuous. And unpopular, I'm afraid. None of the ladies wants to be seen with someone as hopelessly out of step as I am."

Though he made his voice mournful she could see the glint of mischief in his eyes. "Well, if you're looking for sympathy, don't look here," she retorted. She tried to tug her fingers away—though she didn't try very hard. "I find it difficult to believe that with lines like that, you'd be unpopular with the ladies in any century—hair or no hair."

He grinned. "Thank you—I think."

And then the grin faded; he linked his fingers with hers and raised their entwined hands a few inches off the bed, gazing at them absently. "You know, it's funny. Most of my life, all I've wanted is to be a part of the twentieth century. My entire career has been devoted to studying it, and I'm never more comfortable than when I'm actually here, in this time. I could be perfectly content living out a full life here— that's all I've ever wanted to do, really. But now the most important work of my life, the *hardest* work of my life, is spent trying to figure out a way to leave it behind."

She felt a catch in her throat, and her fingers tightened involuntarily on his. But she couldn't dwell on that. She couldn't.

Instead, she asked, "Have you ever been here before—in the nineties?"

He shook his head. "I like to do my work chronologically. I had just finished an overview of the seventies, and was beginning the eighties. Of course, the nineties are in many ways the most exciting decade—certainly the most tumultuous—of the century. I'm glad I got to see it."

He brought their linked hands to his face then, where he caressed the backs of her fingers briefly with his cheek, and then to his chest, resting them just above the beat of his heart. Houston did not object. She let the quietness of the night and the warmth of the moment draw them together and seal them in.

"What's it like—three hundred years from now? Is life better? Is society stronger? Is the future worth waiting for?" *And are all the men like you? Because if so, there is hope for us all....*

He chose his answer carefully, as of course he would. "In many ways it's better. Certainly everyday life is simpler, with all the modern conveniences we have."

Houston stifled a surprised giggle. She considered herself fairly well equipped in the modern-convenience department, but she supposed her household must seem as backward to him as a pioneer woman's sod house would to her.

"We don't work as many hours to provide for our families as you do now," he went on. "I suppose that's good. Women and children are society's most valuable assets, and they are treated as such. Crimes against the innocent are almost nonexistent." His tone was a little nostalgic—and something more.

"Wow," Houston said softly. "I could live there."

"There is a price to be paid for these advances in civilization, however—there always is. I think sometimes we have less freedom than you do. I know we have fewer choices. And—" he smiled at her "—our lives are not nearly as exciting as yours."

"Exciting? Surely you don't mean my life."

"Every time you get behind the wheel of an automobile, every time you stand in front of a classroom, every time you go into a supermarket, you experience an adventure most people of my time can't even imagine. There's an amusement park called Freeways of the Twenty-First Century—traffic gets much worse before it gets better, I should warn you—and people flock to it by the thousands to have a taste of the excitement of these times.''

Houston laughed. "I'm not sure whether I believe you, but you have given me a new appreciation of rush hour."

His skin was smooth and warm against her hand, the muscles of his chest firm. She could feel the rhythmic rise and fall with his breath, and she wanted to open her fingers, to spread her hand over that strong, masculine expanse, caressing and exploring. Perhaps he saw it in her eyes. Something about the tenderness of his smile, a slight softening of his gaze, made her drop her own eyes as she searched for a more neutral topic.

"What other centuries have you studied?" she asked in a moment.

"None," he admitted. "It takes years of study to learn the customs and details of a particular time period, and then of course there's the language problem. Once you choose an area of specialization, you stick with it."

"Language?"

He nodded, smiling. "Anything past the twenty-first century is an entirely alien language to us. Except for variations in dialect, we speak a single planetary language now—and most of it, interestingly enough, is based on what Mark would call 'compuspeak.'"

Houston's brow creased with a puzzled frown. "What's that?"

"The shorthand computer bulletin board and E-mail users are inventing even now—and for the record, that's something no one knew until I discovered it, working with Mark. The origins of an entire language rediscovered…that's quite a find, and it'll be sure to set the academic world on its ear when I…"

The glow of excitement that had begun to kindle in his eyes faded as they both realized what he had been about to say. Houston's fingers tightened on his, and she said a little more intensely than she had intended, "I don't understand. I know history is important. I know we all need to know where we came from to know who we are. But it *can't* be this important. Not enough to risk your life for."

"The men and women of your time are risking their lives to explore space, and they do so with much less promise of reward than we have. You see, it's not just abstracts we've lost, but technology, botanicals—things that could make a real difference in our lives if they could be applied to the problems of the twenty-fourth century. It is important," he assured her, and his eyes showed no fear, no regret. "It is worth dying for."

Houston closed her eyes against the pain that was slowly twisting in her chest. It was a moment before she could speak.

"Mark..." She had to clear her throat. "Mark doesn't think it's going very well."

"No," he admitted, holding her gaze. "Not through any fault of his or his bulletin-board friends who are helping. The problem is we're about six years too early for even the simplest piece of technology I need."

"But..." Her throat constricted with anxiety. "You can improvise, right? You can invent what you need, or alter something we already have..."

"It's not very likely."

The look in his eyes was patient and apologetic, watchful and sad. From it she knew what he was going to say before he spoke.

"Houston, I may have to ask you to do some things for me. There are arrangements that should be made and—"

"No!" She jerked her hand away. "No, I don't want to hear that. You're talking like you've given up and you can't give up! There is a way—there has to be!"

"I haven't given up. But we have to face reality, and be prepared for the worst."

But Houston couldn't. She couldn't face the possibility of failure, not if it meant his life. Even though success would take him away from her, at least she would know that somewhere, in some *time,* he lived.

She half turned from him, pressing her lips tightly to close off the words she had no right to say—or perhaps to just silence the sobs.

Quinn sat up, taking her shoulders gently from behind. "I'm sorry. I know I have no right to ask anything of you. I've brought so much turmoil into your life and Mark's already. Believe me, if I could take it back, I would."

"It's just that—it's so unfair, you know?" Houston's voice sounded tight and high, and she focused her eyes on the corner where the ceiling met the wall. "I mean . . . I'm almost thirty-three years old, and in all that time you're the only good thing, besides my son, that's ever happened to me. The only one."

His hands tightened on her shoulders, but he said nothing.

"I know you don't belong here, I know there's no, well, future for us, so to speak . . ." She even tried to smile. "And that's bad enough, but given the history of my relationship with men—if it weren't for bad luck, I wouldn't have any luck at all—it's not surprising. I hate it. But . . . if you go back . . . at least I can think of you, now and then, and daydream about . . . possibilities . . ."

She was beginning to choke up; she fought back the tears deliberately. "But if you don't go back, then it's over, tragically, finally. And all I'll ever be able to think about is that because you came here, and loved me—because you were a part of our lives for this tiny little space of time—you died. You never got to be what you were supposed to be in your own time, you never got to live out your life the way you were meant to, you never got to think back, and remember me...."

Her voice was harshened now, by tears and anger, and her hands closed into tight fists. "That makes me angry, Quinn. So don't ask me to talk about what has to be done. Don't ask me to be prepared for the worst. I know you're right. I know we have to deal with these things. But not now. Now, just let me be angry."

His hands caressed her shoulders, tenderly gathering her to him, even as he bent his head to bury his face in her hair. "Ah, Houston." His breath was warm on her neck. "If I could live a thousand years, I could never make up for the pain I've caused you."

He raised his face and let his hands slip down her arms, cupping her elbows. "I want to tell you something. I wasn't going to raise false hopes. But now I want you to know."

Houston turned around and looked at him."

"All the effort I've put into trying to get back, instead of trying to find a way to stay here safely—it wasn't because I wanted to leave you."

"I know that," she protested quickly, but he laid a finger lightly across her lips to silence her.

"It was because I knew that only by going back could I find a way to stay with you. You see," he explained, "even though we can only stay in a foreign century a few weeks at a time because of the limitations of the serum, we *can* return to our own time, detoxify our systems and then travel back in time again—*arriving only a few minutes after we left.* That's how I was able to spend almost a whole summer with Sam, and he never knew I had ever left.''

Houston's heart began to beat faster as she understood the implications.

Then he said, ''Unfortunately, we can only do this a few times before the magnetic pattern begins to wear thin, preventing us from returning to the same time period at all. But research is being done on the problems every day. If I could get back to my own time, I could find a way to make it possible for a traveler to stay indefinitely in a foreign time. Then I would come back to you . . . if you wanted me.''

Her heartbeat caught, tumbled, raced—and only partially from hope, desperate though it might be. The joy that filled her chest and made her light-headed was simply from knowing that he had formulated a plan and wanted it to work.

''It could take a long time,'' she said.

''You would never know I was gone.''

''You would be older.''

He hesitated, then nodded, dropping his eyes. ''Probably.''

Houston smiled. Lifting her hand to his face, she lightly touched one corner of his mouth. ''You might be bald.''

She felt the curve of his smile beneath her fingertip before he lifted his eyes. ''I might,'' he agreed. ''Do you think you could learn to like that?''

''I might.''

He captured her hand, kissing her fingers.

"You might forget about me," Houston said softly. "You might go back to your own time and find someone else."

Quinn's eyes were dark and serious. "There is no one else," he said simply. "In my time, a man has only one mate. You are mine."

Tears trembled on Houston's lashes, blurring his face in a mist of tenderness and need. She said, only a little thickly, "Now I want to tell you something. Whatever happens, you'll always be my hero."

Placing her hands on either side of his face, she leaned forward and kissed him gently.

She pulled away, and they looked at each other for a moment. His hand caressed her hair, cupping the back of her neck. His eyes absorbed her. She felt him inside her, mingling with her soul. She felt him in her breath, in her heartbeat. She felt as though, if she simply relaxed her muscles, she would flow into him, become a part of him, inseparable forever. And that was what she did.

Leaning forward, she let her weight press him back onto the bed, settling her legs on either side of him, her skirt falling over them like a curtain. She took his lower lip between her teeth, lightly nibbling, tasting him. His hands gathered up her hair, entwining his fingers through it, then combing it free, tugging out the curls. She pressed her palms to his chest, kissing his nipples, tracing the shape of his muscles. He slipped his hands beneath the fall of her skirt, caressing her calves and the curve of her knee and her thighs. His palms cupped her buttocks, fingers hooking inside the elastic band of her panties. He kissed her face.

"I love your freckles," he murmured. "They taste like sunshine."

She pushed her fingers into his hair, a smile of sheer pleasure spreading across her face as she kissed his throat. "I love your hair. Don't be a slave to fashion."

He tugged her panties down, straightening her legs to remove them. Houston reached between their bodies and unsnapped his jeans, slid down the zipper, then sat back to help him tug the material free of his hips.

Their breathing, now deep and heavy, was as one. They kissed, opening their mouths, tasting deeply of each other. Their hands joined, fingers locked, arm muscles stretching. As naturally as night becoming day, they merged and became one.

Their lovemaking was sweet, like a sonnet, and tumultuous, like a storm. They wrapped themselves around each other and drew themselves into each other, straining together, swelling together, poised together for one endless suspended moment on the edge of rapture, then bursting together into a thousand fragments of glittering pleasure; she and he, mixed and inextricable, not one part distinguishable from the other.

They lay in a damp tangle of arms and legs and twisted clothing, heartbeats and breathing gradually slowing, the fever fading. But the glow that surrounded them did not fade; the intensity that joined them did not diminish. Outside, the moon rose and stars came out, the crickets began their familiar song. Inside, they lay together in silence, holding each other and treasuring the moment.

"Take me with you," Houston whispered. She lifted her head, looking at him. "I can't take the chance on letting you go—that something might go wrong again. You've got to find a way to rebuild the resonator and take Mark and me with you."

He combed his fingers through her hair, his expression gentle and sad. "I can't. Even if I had the technology, you couldn't survive in my time, any more than I can now survive in yours."

Houston lowered her head to his chest, biting her lip against further protests.

Quinn wrapped both arms around her, kissing her hair, holding her tightly. "I'll find a way," he promised her, his voice low and hoarse. "I'll survive this, I'll go home and I'll come back to you. I have to."

Chapter Twelve

"Mom! Quinn!"

It was ten o'clock the next morning. She and Quinn were finishing breakfast; Mark had bolted his and run off somewhere almost half an hour earlier. It was promising to be a perfect June day, soft and lazy and bathed in sunshine. But neither the bright morning light that flowed through the bay window nor the glow of warmth that lingered between them last night could disguise the mauve circles beneath Quinn's eyes or the tired, grayish color of his skin. Houston was worried about him. She didn't want to tell him so, but she was.

They both looked around when Mark burst through the kitchen door, sweaty and flushed and looking as though he had run an obstacle course to reach them. His hair was tangled with twigs and briars, his cheeks were smudged and his hands were filthy, and the knees of his jeans were coated with mud. Such a hapless disregard for cleanliness might have been typical for any other ten-year-old boy, but for her son it was definitely a cause for remark.

"Mark!" exclaimed Houston in dismay. "Look at you! Where have you been? How did you get so filthy?"

He stood just inside the doorway, breathing hard, his face alight with triumph and excitement. "It was so simple," he said, looking at Quinn. "I don't know why we didn't see it before!"

Houston got up from the table and went to the sink, snatching up a handful of paper towels and dampening them under the faucet before offering them to her son. Mark ignored them. Quinn, apparently sensing something Houston did not, regarded Mark intently.

"I retraced your steps that first morning," Mark explained. "Everything—the apple tree, the fall, the argument with Mom—"

"I did that," Quinn interrupted. "That first day, after you and your mother left for school, I went over everything in my mind, I retraced every step—"

"But you forgot Arthur!" Mark exclaimed.

Quinn frowned. "Who?"

"The dog! Arthur, the sheepdog—he lives next door! Remember? He was running around, knocking into things—"

"He stepped on some of my equipment," Quinn said slowly, his expression distracted as he remembered. "And then you came and held him . . ."

"And then he got away," finished Mark excitedly. "And none of us were watching him by then. So last night I was thinking, and I remembered how Arthur likes to hide his toys under the toolshed at his house...."

Houston let the sodden wad of paper towels fall unused into the sink. She could feel her heart actually leap in her chest as her son reached into his back pocket and triumphantly pulled out a small metal case that looked like nothing more than a pocket calculator.

"So I went there and I found this," he said. "This is it, isn't it, Quinn? It's the resonator!"

Houston knew by the way the color drained from Quinn's face, by the way that he slowly rose from his chair, that Mark was right. She sank back against the counter, her knees suddenly weak.

Quinn went over to Mark and took the instrument from him. Then he dropped to his knees and hugged Mark. Houston's eyes blurred and she had to close them, offering up a brief, deeply powerful prayer of gratitude.

When she opened her eyes, Mark was grinning, so puffed up with pride that he looked as though he might take flight at any moment. Quinn was examining the resonator with wonder and barely subdued excitement in his eyes. "It's been damaged," he said, his voice low and quick, "but I don't think it's beyond repair. Mark..."

He looked up, and though Houston could not see exactly what passed between the two males with that look, she knew it was something her son would carry with him the rest of his life. "Thank you," Quinn said simply.

And then he added, "Now go upstairs and get cleaned up. I can't say for sure, but I can just about bet a trip to Radio Shack will be called for before this day is over."

Mark ran toward the stairs, and Houston just stood there, her hands pressed to her hot cheeks, hardly daring to release the laugh of delight that was bubbling up inside her. Quinn, still on his knees, turned to look at her, and her own amazement and joy was reflected on his face.

"I don't believe it," he said.

"So simple," she agreed.

He looked at the resonator in his hand, and then he looked at her. He got to his feet—and his face went chalk white. He grasped the back of a chair to keep from falling. Houston rushed to him, slipping her arm around his waist. The bubbling excitement that had buoyed her only a moment ago was now a cold weight of fear in her stomach.

"Are you all right?" she demanded. "Quinn!"

"No—it's okay. I'm okay." He passed a hand through his hair, and Houston noticed it was trembling. He took a few deep breaths, though, and after a moment, when he looked at her, his smile seemed genuine.

He put his arms around her, wrapping her in his embrace, holding her close. "Oh, Houston," he said. "It's possible. Now . . . it's possible."

For the first time, she believed it was.

THEY MADE TWO TRIPS to computer stores for parts that Quinn could break down and redesign for his own purpose before stopping at Radio Shack for the tools Quinn would need to begin his work.

"I won't be able to determine the full extent of the damage until I open it," Quinn said. "But as long as the magnetic field is intact, I can improvise everything else."

"Sounds dangerous," Houston said.

Quinn just grinned. "Isn't everything?"

Houston slipped her arm through his and squeezed it briefly, happy because he was, and because the pallor had almost disappeared from his cheeks.

The salesman who approached them looked nervous. "Hi, Mark," he said. He glanced at Quinn, then at Houston, then at Mark again. "Anything in particular today?"

"Nah, Quinn knows what he wants."

"Oh, yes." The clerk smiled at Quinn, but there was something a little strained about it. "You were here before, weren't you?"

Quinn nodded. "I need a voltage tester and some wire clips."

"Right this way."

"That's okay—I see them."

The salesman looked a little disconcerted, then turned quickly back to Mark. "We just got the upgrade for Battlestar. You want to try it out?"

"We're in kind of a hurry," Houston said.

"It's got the speech package," the salesclerk said persuasively.

Mark looked hopefully at his mother. "It'll just take a minute."

It took more than a minute. While the young clerk was busy demonstrating the intergalactic features of the new game to Mark, the sales manager went over to Quinn, offering all kinds of helpful advice that Houston could tell by the expression on Quinn's face was not very helpful at all, and engaging him in a long conversation about a project he was working on at home. Quinn kept trying to move away politely, impatience evident on his face, until finally Houston felt compelled to intercede.

She came over to him and glanced pointedly at her watch. "We really should be going if we don't want to be late," she said.

"You're right," agreed Quinn. He glanced at his nemesis. "Excuse me. We have an appointment."

The sales manager said cheerfully, "Let me ring you up, then."

Houston called to Mark and they went to the counter.

The total was $12.49. Quinn paid with a ten and a five. The sales manager looked at the bills as though he didn't know what they were for a moment, then he flashed Quinn a smile. "I hate to ask, but would you happen to have a twenty? We're running low on bigger bills and need to get rid of some of our change."

Quinn reached into his wallet and handed over a twenty. The salesman looked at the bill and swallowed hard. He looked over the cash register, at something behind them, and it was in that split second that Houston realized something was wrong.

Her insight came too late, however, although it was unlikely that any amount of forewarning could have prevented what happened next. When Houston turned to Quinn, two policemen were there, one on either side of him. One of them said, "Just hold it right there, if you would, please, sir."

Two men in suits—presumably detectives—went behind the counter to the salesman, who said, "This is it. Just like the other one we got." He was holding up the bill Quinn had just paid with.

Through the glass front of the store Houston could see two police cars parked. A third one was just pulling up, dome light flashing. Instinctively she put her arm around Mark and pulled him close even as she demanded, "What is this? What is going on?"

One of the detectives addressed Quinn. "I don't suppose you noticed anything unusual about this twenty-dollar bill, now, did you?"

He held the bill out to Quinn to examine, but Quinn hardly glanced at it. "Like what?"

"Like the date, for instance—1998?"

Houston felt a sinking feeling low in her stomach. Her eyes met Quinn's, and the look of horror that passed between them must have seemed like one of guilt. The two uniformed officers shifted subtly closer to Quinn and placed their hands on their holsters. The detective, cold-eyed, said, "I'm Raymond Sharp from the United States Treasury Department. Could I see some identification, please?"

"IN OTHER NEWS, a Carsonville man was arrested today for counterfeiting."

Houston watched numbly as the image of the pretty brunette anchor gave way to a photograph of Quinn, side profile and full face. "Identified as David Quinn of Clarion, Minnesota, he is accused of distributing more than a thousand dollars' worth of phony twenties from his base in Carsonville over the past month. Authorities say the bills are virtually undetectable as frauds except for one minor detail... the date of printing is 1998. If you are in possession of any of the bills—"

Houston hit the mute button on the remote control and turned back to her telephone conversation. "Look, there's got to be something you can do."

The lawyer to whom Millie had recommended her—Millie, God bless her, was the kind of friend who would help first and ask questions later—was sympathetic but firm. "I've done everything I could, but there's no way we can move the arraignment up any sooner than tomorrow afternoon. Even so, I've got to tell you the chances are bail will be denied. The man has no job, no roots in the community, a strong motive to flee and the means to do so. I'll make an argument, but I've got to tell you, it just doesn't look good."

Houston twisted the telephone cord around her wrist, half turning from the living room, where Mark was watching and listening intently to every word she said. She lowered her voice. "Listen. You've got to get him out of there. I don't care what it takes, he's got to get out. He's...he's not well. He can't stay there."

"Well, we can get a doctor to him tonight if he needs one. But beyond that—"

"What he needs is to go home!"

A reproachful silence followed her outburst. Houston drew a calming breath, but it wasn't calming at all. They were so close. How could this be happening?

In a quieter tone, she asked, "Can you at least arrange for me to see him tonight?"

She had spent almost six hours answering police questions herself...and all the time she kept thinking about the collection of bills Quinn had given her for rent that were hidden away in her savings bank, and thanking whatever fates were responsible that she had not spent any of them. If both she and Quinn were in jail, they would be helpless.

By the time she was allowed to leave the police station, visiting hours at the jail were over, and she had spent the next several hours on the telephone, back and forth with the lawyer. She wanted to let Quinn know she had not deserted him. She wanted to tell him everything was going to be all right.

But was it?

The lawyer answered, "Visiting hours start at ten in the morning. No exceptions. I'm sorry. I'll be by to talk to him before the arraignment, and then you and I should meet tomorrow afternoon. Say about four, at my office?"

Knowing there was nothing else she could do, Houston agreed and hung up the phone.

Mark looked at her from across the room, sober and big-eyed. She didn't know what to say to him.

He was the one who finally spoke. "Pretty bad, huh, Mom?"

Houston nodded, once again swallowing back a lump of fear and defeat. How could this have happened?

But she managed a smile, which, if it wasn't convincing, was at least brave. "Nothing we can't handle, though," she said. She sat down beside Mark and put an arm around his shoulders, hugging him. "It's going to be fine. You'll see."

She only wished she could believe that.

"IT WAS STUPID," Quinn said. "It's my fault and I have no excuses. I should have checked the bills. I knew the equipment had been damaged and I should have checked."

The Carsonville jail was small and provided no formal visitors' room. Houston was escorted to the cell area, where she and Quinn were forced to conduct their conversation in low voices, separated by bars.

He looked awful. They had taken his clothes and given him a standard-issue blue cotton jumpsuit. Houston hated that. She knew it was common procedure, but it made his incarceration look so permanent. His hair was rumpled and he was hollow-eyed from lack of sleep; his skin was damp and sallow. Houston put her hand atop his fingers, which were curled around one of the bars.

"How did it happen?" she asked quietly.

He gave a small shake of his head, signifying nothing by the gesture except his own impatience with himself. "I have a machine that produces some of the necessities for survival outside our own time— documents, money, things like that. The bills aren't counterfeit," he insisted. "Technically, they're perfectly legitimate—or they will be in 1998. Apparently the equipment was malfunctioning just enough to print the wrong twenties. I should have checked."

Houston nodded thoughtfully. "Not much of a defense, though."

He brought his forehead to rest against the bars. "I'm sorry, Houston. Once again, I've brought you nothing but trouble."

Houston caressed his brow and was alarmed by how hot it felt. "Quinn, we've got to get you out of here. You look ill, and I think you have a fever."

He shook his head and straightened up. "I'm fine. I didn't sleep, that's all. Not that I'm disagreeing—I need to get out of here. I just can't think how, right now. As you pointed out, my defense is a little weak."

He passed his hand, palm up, through the bars, and she placed her hand inside it. "How's Mark?" he inquired with concern.

"He insisted on coming with me. They wouldn't let him in, of course. He's waiting in the car."

"This is going to be embarrassing for him," Quinn said heavily. "And for you. The publicity will be unavoidable, and none of it will reflect kindly on you."

Houston gave an impatient shake of her head. "We'll deal with that when the time comes. For now we've got more important problems."

He stroked her cheek, smiling tenderly. "What did I do to deserve you?"

"Is there anything Mark and I can do," she inquired anxiously, "about the resonator? If we brought it to you, and the tools, could you . . . ?"

The big metal door that separated the prisoners from the jailors creaked open and slammed shut, cutting off Houston's words. A rather chubby policewoman came through, followed by a sleek, dark-haired woman in a gray business suit.

The policewoman said, "David Quinn?"

She came up to the cell door, key in hand, and Houston stepped away. "The charges against you have been dropped, Mr. Quinn," the policewoman said. "You're free to go. Please stop by the desk to claim your personal belongings."

Houston stared at her. "Dropped? But how—"

The other woman stepped forward briskly and extended her hand to Quinn. "I'm Morgan, your attorney. I know we haven't officially met, but I thought it was best to get this nonsense out of the way first."

The woman had a throaty voice and a powerful, businesslike manner that left no doubt in anyone's mind who was in charge. But the lawyer Houston had hired was a man.

She said, confused, "Are you an associate of Mr. Carruthers?"

The woman glanced at her in thinly disguised irritation, then looked back at Quinn. "Why don't I explain it on the way out?"

The policewoman had already reached the metal door and was waiting for them to join her. Quinn left the cell, letting Morgan usher him toward the door. When Houston started to say something else, he silenced her with a look, and she had to agree: it would be foolish to look a gift horse in the mouth. Although the last thing Morgan, with her dark exotic beauty, resembled was a horse.

Quinn changed into his street clothes and signed the form for the return of his possessions. Before he put his wallet away, he opened it and counted the money. What he found was not evident on his face as they left the building.

"It's all there," he said quietly to Morgan as he pushed open the door to the vestibule.

She replied, "I should certainly hope so."

"Even the twenties."

Now Houston was beginning to catch on. "They should have been evidence."

The three of them stood inside the small glass-enclosed foyer, which was already beginning to heat up from the summer sun. Despite the fact, Houston felt a cold prickle at the base of her neck.

Morgan met Quinn's eyes. "I think you'll find that the dates on those twenties are now entirely correct. Charges were dropped, after all, for lack of evidence."

Quinn said very deliberately, "You changed history."

And Morgan smiled. "No," she answered, "only the dates on a few twenty-dollar bills."

Houston was finding it increasingly difficult to catch her breath in the small, close space. She could see the beads of sweat on Quinn's face, the disturbing dilation of his pupils. He couldn't take his eyes off Morgan. Neither could Houston, after that last statement.

It was Houston who regained her voice first. "You're . . . from Quinn's time period?"

Morgan glanced at her, obviously startled.

"No," Quinn said. "Not from my time."

Morgan seemed to make a decision. She turned to Quinn, straightened her shoulders and looked him in the eye. She said, "My year is 2382, approximately seventy-five years after your disappearance. Sir, it is truly an honor to meet you. I have come to take you home."

Quinn leaned back against the glass wall in a gesture that almost appeared casual. But Houston saw the perspiration trickle down his cheek, and she saw that he had difficulty swallowing. She moved closer to him, touching his arm.

"Let's go outside," she suggested.

But Quinn did not appear to hear her. He seemed to be aware of no one except Morgan. "How," he demanded hoarsely, "did you find me?"

She smiled. "We can capture broadcast beams with one-hundred-percent accuracy now. No one else need ever risk his life in time travel to bring our past back to us. We saw the news of your arrest on one of our satellite transmissions, and it solved a seventy-five-year-old mystery for us. The plan to rescue you has been ten years in the making, but we finally made it work."

Quinn looked as stunned as Houston felt. He pushed an unsteady hand through his hair, as though struggling to clear his thoughts. "And you can do that—take me back to my own time?"

Morgan smiled and extended her hand to him. "I can do that," she said. "That's why I'm here."

Quinn smiled, too, but it was a little wavery. "Well," he said. "If that's the case, then all I can say is, it's about time."

He gestured toward the door, indicating they should precede him. Morgan pushed open the door first, and Houston followed.

Quinn took two steps toward them, and collapsed.

Chapter Thirteen

Houston paced back and forth before the big picture window in the hospital waiting room, hugging her arms tightly, trying to breathe steadily. "Why is it taking so long?" she demanded of no one in particular. "Why won't they come talk to us?"

Because they can't leave him, another voice said inside her head. *Because he's strapped to life-support equipment and they don't know whether his next breath will be his last... because he's comatose and they can't bring him out of it... because he's already gone...*

She felt a presence beside her, and Mark reached for her hand. "It's okay, Mom," he said. His voice was clear with the simple conviction of the very young. "He's not going to die, not when he's this close to going home. It doesn't work that way. He's not going to die."

It took Houston a moment to bring her voice under control, to force back the tears that threatened to flood her throat. Because Quinn had looked so pale when they had taken him away on the stretcher. So pale and still. And because the truth was, sometimes it did work that way.

She squeezed her son's hand and managed a smile. "I think you're probably right, Mark. It doesn't seem fair, does it?"

He shook his head soberly. Houston dropped to one knee beside him.

"I think you should know," Houston said quietly, "that Quinn didn't want to leave us, not even to save his life. He had a plan to come back—to solve the problems that they have now with time travel, and to come back, and stay. I don't know whether his plan would have worked," she admitted, "but it was what he wanted."

Mark nodded. "Sure," he said. "Makes sense. It's what I would have done." Then he added, "You guys are in love, aren't you, Mom?"

Her vision blurred with hot tears; to hide it, she hugged her son, squeezing her eyes tightly closed against his T-shirt-clad shoulder. "Yes," she whispered. "Very much."

"Then his plan will work. I'll bet you."

"Excuse me."

Houston recognized the deep contralto voice of the woman called Morgan. She had come with Houston to the emergency room in a stilted, detached silence, had followed them through the admitting procedure and into the waiting room without saying a word and had then taken a seat on the opposite side of the room from Houston, folded her hands in her lap and proceeded to wait. Houston hadn't meant to ignore her, but she hadn't known what to say. In the last agonizing half hour or so, as her anxiety about Quinn grew more consuming, she had almost forgotten about the other woman entirely.

Houston stood up slowly, still holding Mark's hand. She cleared her throat. "Um, Morgan. Is there something I can do for you?"

"I doubt it," she answered. "I confess, I wasn't prepared for this."

Her voice, with its firm no-nonsense intonation, as well as her cool unblinking beauty, made her seem cold, Houston realized, almost disinterested. But she wasn't. There was genuine distress in her eyes, although her strict composure made it difficult to see.

"It occurred to me," she went on, "that if you could tell me something about what Quinn's lifestyle has been since he's been here, perhaps I would have a better chance of diagnosing his illness. You seem to know him rather well, and—" she slanted Houston a quick sideways glance "—if he confided to you where he was really from, he must have confided other things, as well."

She looked at Mark, then at Houston. "Perhaps I haven't been polite. Some of the nuances of your culture still elude me. I don't, for example, believe I know your name."

"My name is Houston Malloy. This is my son, Mark."

Morgan looked again at Mark, and something flickered in her eyes—something that was very close to surprise, or even excitement. "Mark Malloy?"

Mark said, "Yes, ma'am."

A slow, vaguely wondering smile spread over Morgan's face. "Mark Malloy," she said softly. "Of course. You would be a child now. We always wondered how—" But then she cut herself off; the smile vanished as abruptly as though a switch had been thrown. "Well, I'm sure that's not appropriate."

She looked back at Houston. "I should explain. The design of this rescue has required some of the most brilliant minds of my time. We thought we had virtually eliminated the possibility of failure. To have this happen—" She stopped and cleared her throat, and seemed for a moment to struggle with an emotion. Then she finished simply, "You see, in my time, Quinn is a legend. A hero."

Houston touched her arm in a brief gesture of comfort. "In my time, too," she said softly.

A male voice spoke behind them. "Excuse me. I'm looking for the family of David Quinn."

Houston turned quickly to face the doctor, her heartbeat seizing with anxiety. "I'm Houston Malloy," she said.

"And I'm Dr. Morgan," Morgan said abruptly, striding toward the doctor with her hand extended. "I'm here as a friend of the family. Please tell me all you can about the patient's condition."

The doctor shook Morgan's hand, glancing from her to Houston. Then he said, gesturing to a group of chairs by the window. "Why don't we all sit down?"

The heavy weight in Houston's chest did not ease as they were seated, and the doctor began to speak. "Mr. Quinn is a very sick man. And I'm sorry to say we don't know why. He seems to be suffering from a massive infection—his temperature is a hundred and four, leukocytes and erythrocites are elevated. He's beginning to develop a pitecheal rash that could be symptomatic of rubella or scarlet fever—or a dozen other more exotic illnesses." He looked at Houston. "It would help me to know if he's been out of the country in the last month or so."

How about out of the century? Houston thought, but she shook her head. "No."

The doctor addressed Morgan. "In addition, his system seems to be demonstrating a noticeable histaminic reaction. We're scanning for known toxins and doing a drug analysis just in case. Most of the blood cultures will take forty-eight hours, but you might be interested in the gram stains."

From the clipboard he carried he pulled out several sheets of paper to which were affixed yellow lab sheets. Morgan looked through them without comment.

"Right now we're pushing fluids and a broad-spectrum antibiotic. Until we know more, that's all we can do."

"Can we see him?"

The doctor looked as though he would refuse Houston's request out of hand, and then his expression softened. "He's under sedation now. Give us a few hours. We'll see."

When the doctor was gone, Houston turned to Morgan urgently. "Can you help him? Surely in your time you must know a way to treat these things."

But Morgan just shook her head, her expression one of bafflement. "These bacteria that are showing up on the tests, these diseases—they are all from your century. That shouldn't be. How could he be susceptible to these things?"

Houston leaned her head back, unable to continue to hold her shoulders straight against the weight of defeat that was pressing down on them. "The serum," she said. "When he realized he wasn't going to be able to get back before he ran out, he started cutting the doses in half."

For the first time genuine shock was reflected in Morgan's face, making her look almost animated. "But...that's impossible! He wouldn't have done anything so reckless! He'll die!"

"He had no choice," Houston returned. "He took a chance. Don't people in your time ever do that?"

Morgan just stared at her. "No," she said.

Mark spoke up. "Ms.—uh—Morgan. Maybe if you could go down to the lab," he suggested, "and— I don't know—scope it out or something, you might get an idea of what we have to work with and figure out a way to help Quinn.''

Morgan looked at him thoughtfully. "That's a sensible suggestion," she agreed. "I'll need the accoutrements of the profession."

Houston looked at Mark and he interpreted. "A lab coat. One of those clipboards. Maybe a stethoscope. I saw a supply closet when we came in. I'll be right back."

HOUSTON DIDN'T KNOW whether Morgan would be able to do anything for Quinn, but it was a relief to have her out of the way, to be released from the scrutiny of that cold gaze. If she was representative of women of the future, it was no wonder Quinn preferred to live in the past.

As the day wore on, she curled up in a corner of the sofa and stared out the window and thought about destiny. The odd twist of fate that had brought Quinn into her grandfather's life sixty years ago. The "accident" that had landed him in her apple tree so many years and miles later. The absurdity with misprinted twenty-dollar bills when Quinn was so close to safety—yet if he had not been arrested, there would have been no story about him on the evening news, and the people of the future would never have known what had become of him. Morgan would have never come back to help him.

Fate had gone out of its way to bring Quinn into her life. How could it take him from her now?

Toward sunset, Mark fell asleep on the sofa beside her. Houston, exhausted from the strain of the past days, was beginning to doze herself when she felt the firm grip of a hand on her shoulder. She started awake.

For a moment she didn't recognize Morgan, who was dressed in surgical greens and a paper cap, with a mask dangling around her neck. "Quinn is awake," she said. "He has asked to see you." She thrust a packet of green clothes similar to the ones she wore toward Houston. "Put these on over your clothes. They are trying to maintain an isolation barrier." She lifted one shoulder in a gesture of resignation. "Their efforts are pitiable, of course, but they do the best they can within the limits of their knowledge."

Houston got up without disturbing Mark and pulled on the baggy pants and shirt over her jeans. "How is he?" she asked quietly.

"He has pneumonia," Morgan said. "I don't recall—is that a curable disease in your time?"

Houston stuffed her hair under the paper hat, allowing her to feel some hope. "Sometimes. Most of the time."

"Your physicians are puzzled. He seems to be succumbing to and curing himself of a remarkable number of diseases, one after another. In light of the effect of the serum, even at half dose, this is logical. But the science of your time has no explanation for it."

Houston tied the mask around her neck. "But that's good! That means he's going to be all right, doesn't it?"

Morgan's expression did not change, but Houston thought she saw a slight shake of her head. "He's very weak" was her only answer.

Houston caught her arm. "There has to be something you can do for him. You can transport him back to your time and bring medicine, or a specialist. You can—"

"The medicines of my time would be poison to him. We have no cure for these diseases. The battle to survive in your century is one that must be fought by him alone."

HOUSTON PUSHED OPEN the door to Quinn's room silently, followed closely by Morgan. Quinn's eyes were closed, his face pale except for the flush of fever, but when he opened his eyes, Houston felt a rush of hope. She hurried to him, taking his hand in both of hers.

He smiled weakly. "The medical facilities of your time are barbarous," he murmured.

His voice was hoarse. She could feel the strain every breath cost him. "You're doing better, Quinn. Morgan says you're fighting off the infection."

He shook his head tiredly. "It was an insane idea. I never should have decreased the dosage."

"You had no choice," Houston said firmly.

"Is Morgan here?"

It was becoming harder for him to speak as his breath grew shorter. Houston tightened her grip on his hand, trying to infuse him with strength.

Morgan stepped forward. "I'm here."

Quinn moved his eyes from Houston to Morgan. He said with an effort, "I never went back. In the original history, I died in the twentieth century."

Morgan said nothing. Houston convulsively tightened her hands around Quinn's.

The faintest trace of a smile hovered on Quinn's lips as he told Morgan, "You can't change history. We both know that. But thanks . . . for trying."

"Stop it!" Houston commanded. "Stop talking like that. You're getting better. You are!"

Quinn turned his gaze back to her. Lifting his hand, he touched her cheek, lightly brushing the dampness away. "I've let you down," he said softly. "I'm sorry. I try never to make promises I can't keep."

Houston caught his hand and kissed his fingers. "You haven't let me down. You're not going to."

"In my room you'll find quite a bit of money . . ." And again he tried to smile. "Most of it is negotiable in your time."

She began to shake her head furiously but he ignored her. "I made certain there would be enough . . . in case of something like this. It . . . will make your life a little easier. Mark . . ." He had to stop a moment to catch his breath. "Mark will need a superior education. That requires money."

Houston said thickly, "I don't have to listen to this."

"Don't argue with me, Houston. I can't...fight back right now."

Again he had to stop to catch his breath. Houston pressed her forehead against their entwined hands, squeezing her eyes tightly shut. Hot tears slipped through her lashes, anyway.

In a moment Quinn went on. "The picture...in my wallet. Of Sam and me. I want you to have it. Everything else...must be destroyed. Morgan will take care of that. And then..."

He tugged at her hand, making her look at him. "You must forget me."

She shook her head angrily, her voice thick. "You can't make me do that."

Quinn spread his fingers along the side of her face, caressing. "Then remember this. You were the best part of my life, Houston. I wouldn't have missed this for the world."

Houston stretched her arm across his chest, embracing him, and rested her face on the pillow next to his. She stayed that way, holding him and trying not to cry, until he fell asleep, and still she stayed until the nurses came and took her away.

THROUGHOUT THE NIGHT and the next day, the reports came in: he had taken a turn for the worse, he was somewhat better, he was delirious, he was holding his own. Morgan, under her guise as a physician—if indeed it was a disguise, for who knew what the woman might be in her own time—was never far from his side, but Houston was not allowed to visit again. Mark slept, and visited the snack bar and leafed through magazines, and had that look on his face that had become so familiar to her since his father had left: the too-old-for-his-age, I'll-take-care-of-you-Mom look. Houston spent most of her time staring out the window, making bargains with fate and wondering how she would ever be able to say goodbye.

Late in the afternoon, she sensed a silent presence beside her and she turned sharply, expecting it to be a doctor with news of the worst. But it was Morgan, and her expression was unreadable, as always. There seemed to be, however, an odd measure of curiosity in her eyes as she said, "You are Quinn's mate."

In my time, Quinn had said, *a man has only one mate.*

Houston lifted her chin and said simply, "Yes." It was the proudest word she had ever spoken.

Morgan dropped her eyes. "I had no way of knowing," she murmured. "This is ... unexpected. I hope I haven't treated you disrespectfully."

Houston was a little taken aback. "Well ... no. I mean—no."

Morgan looked at her again. "This is an important project to us, for many reasons—the rescue of Quinn. But the custom of my time requires me to ask your permission before I take him away. I should have asked sooner," she apologized, "but I had no way of knowing."

Houston just stared at her. "To save his life? Of course you should take him! That's all I've ever wanted—for him to be safe. Even if it's not with me, for him to be safe . . . alive and healthy somewhere. That's all."

Morgan was silent for a long moment, looking at her. "I think it requires a great deal more courage to be a woman in your time than it does in mine," she remarked. Then she said, "Houston, there is something you should know."

"Miss Malloy."

Houston turned around, and this time it was the doctor. Morgan's last words had caused a knot of dread to form in her chest, and she expected the worst—she expected it, but was by no means prepared for it.

The relaxed smile on the doctor's face as he approached the two of them caught her completely off guard.

"Ah, Dr. Morgan," he said. "I've been looking for you."

"I've been in the lab," replied Morgan cautiously. "Has there been a change?"

"Yes, actually," he announced, looking pleased with himself. "I must say this has been the most extraordinary case I've personally ever been involved with, but I think we may have turned the corner—for good, this time. The man has remarkable recuperative powers. His fever's down, and his lungs are clearing, I can't see any further signs of secondary infection. If he continues to improve tonight, I don't see any reason he can't go home in a day or two."

Houston's heart was beating so fast that she could hardly catch her breath. "He's going to be okay?"

"I'd prefer to remain cautious, but the evidence of the past few hours would indicate—yes. He's going to be okay."

Mark exclaimed, beaming, "See, Mom? I told you so!"

"Can we see him?" Houston demanded.

"Well . . ."

But she didn't wait. She grabbed Mark's hand and ran down the corridor. She pushed open the door to Quinn's room and found him sitting up in bed, waiting for them.

Houston stopped at the door, too full of joy to speak. Her hands went to her throat to ease the ache there. He was alive. Except for a few pounds of lost weight and shadows of fatigue under his eyes, he even looked healthy. And he was smiling at her, however ruefully.

Mark said, "Hi, Quinn."

Quinn answered, "Hi, Mark."

"I knew you'd pull through," Mark added, again affecting nonchalance. "We've got a lot of stuff to do."

Quinn kept his eyes on Houston, still smiling. "We sure do."

Houston said shakily, "Don't you ever scare me like that again."

Quinn opened his arms to her. She flew into them.

They held each other tightly, so tightly that it hurt. She felt his breath on her neck and his strength enfolding her, and happiness bubbled up inside until she couldn't contain it; holding his face between her hands, looking into his eyes, she laughed out loud with pure, unadulterated pleasure. Quinn laughed, too, and releasing her a fraction, he beckoned to Mark with one arm. Mark bounced on the bed and they all embraced again and didn't even look around at the sound of the door closing, or of someone discreetly clearing his throat.

The throat clearing came again and Houston reluctantly disentangled herself from the embrace, expecting to see a disapproving doctor or nurse. It was Morgan, and she looked distressed.

"Morgan, it's okay," Houston said, holding Quinn's hand tightly. She couldn't stop smiling. "He's okay. Everything's going to be fine."

"No," Morgan said unhappily, "it's not. That's what I wanted to tell you before."

She took a step closer to the bed, her hands clasped tightly before her, looking at Quinn. "I've been monitoring your test results. While it's true you have developed antibodies for almost every disease and toxin known to this century so that it's highly unlikely you'll ever succumb to the kinds of ill effects you've just experienced . . . you no longer have immunity to the conditions that exist in your time period. And you've become a carrier for several of the deadliest viruses known—viruses that if released into the twenty-fourth century could decimate the population." She took a deep breath, seeming to fortify her strength. "You can never return to your own time," she said. "I'm sorry."

For a moment no one spoke. Then Mark asked, "Do you mean you don't have to leave?"

And Houston asked, "You can survive in this time—but not in your own?"

Quinn smiled, and put an arm around each of them, drawing Mark and Houston close. "What did I tell you, Morgan?" he said with satisfaction. "You can't change history."

Sinking against his chest with the purest contentment she had known for a long time, Houston was very, very glad.

THREE DAYS LATER they took Quinn home from the hospital. Morgan waited until then to make her own departure, claiming she wanted to make sure to be able to include all the details in her report. Houston thought it was because the other woman was merely curious, and because, perhaps, she had discovered a few things about the twentieth century she liked. Morgan had become a lot more human over the past few days.

The discharge nurse escorted them out of the hospital, but Quinn was strong enough to walk to the car. He stood for a moment beside the car, breathing deeply of the fresh air and turning his face toward the sun. Houston loved him more in that moment than she ever had.

Then he ran his hand lightly over the hood of the car and said, "I suppose I'll have to learn to operate one of these things properly if I'm going to stay."

"I suppose you will," Houston agreed, eyes twinkling. "But you won't be doing it today."

She escorted him to the passenger side and opened the door. Mark got in the back seat, and Quinn waited for Morgan to join him.

Morgan shook her head, smiling regretfully. "This is where I leave you."

"You're welcome to stay with us, as long as you're able," Houston said. And she meant it. She had rather grown to like the other woman.

"No," Morgan said, "this time is for you—and Quinn. I won't intrude. Besides, I do have a life waiting for me in the twenty-fourth century—although I must confess, it's not nearly as interesting as yours."

She turned to Quinn. "There were some things of yours I had to destroy. I hope you don't take offense."

Quinn nodded. "I would have insisted on it."

"It has been an honor to know you, sir." She hesitated, then added, "You were the last of your kind, you know."

"No," Quinn answered quietly. "I didn't know that."

Morgan smiled and looked around. "It's rather a shame. This time travel has a lot to recommend it."

"Perhaps the practice will be revived," suggested Quinn.

"I doubt it. There aren't enough men—or women—like you left."

Quinn extended his hand to her. "Thank your people for me. And Morgan—" he clasped both hands over hers "—thank you."

She smiled. "Good luck, sir."

Quinn looked at Houston. "I don't need it," he said. "I've got something better."

Morgan walked with Houston toward the driver's door. But when they reached the back of the car, Houston stopped.

"Morgan . . ." She glanced toward the window, where she could see Quinn and Mark engaged in conversation. She lowered her voice a fraction. "I was wondering . . . When you first met Mark, you said something that puzzled me. Do you know something about his future?"

Morgan smiled. "It would be unethical of me to answer that."

"From what Quinn tells me," Houston answered craftily, "the best adventurers make up their own rules as they go along."

A spark came into Morgan's eyes. "On the other hand, you are his mother. It might be to your advantage to know."

"I'm sure it would." Houston's heart was beating hard.

Morgan said, "The truth is... do you remember I told you we have a way to retrieve television and radio signals now? Without Mark Malloy, we would not be able to do so. In a way, Mark is the reason I am here."

Houston couldn't contain a gasp of delight. "Mark does that? I knew it! He grows up to be a scientist! I knew it!"

Morgan shook her head. "Not a scientist," she corrected. "A writer. A *science-fiction* writer. His books are classics in my time, mostly because of their prophetic nature. No one has ever been able to adequately explain why he addressed the subjects that he did—time travel, for instance—or how he knew we would one day need a method to recover our past. But it was his theories, which were presented so clearly in fiction, that inspired the research that eventually led to our discovering what happened to Quinn—and coming back to rescue him."

"So," Houston said softly, turning back to look at the two men—*her* two men—through the car window. "He did change history, after all."

"Did he?" Morgan smiled. "Maybe it was simply meant to be."

Houston leaned forward and embraced the other woman. "Goodbye, Morgan."

"I am honored to have known you," she answered. "I shall never forget you."

Houston got into the car and closed the door. But when she looked back to wave one last goodbye to Morgan, the other woman was already gone.

She turned to Quinn and looked at him long and lovingly. "Life," she said, "is fascinating."

Quinn slipped a hand around the back of her neck, stroking. "That it is."

From the back seat, Mark said in mild disgust, "You guys aren't going to start kissing, are you?"

Houston laughed, and Quinn leaned across to kiss her on the lips. "Of course not," he said.

Houston returned his kiss, and Mark groaned.

Houston started the engine, grinning. "Ready?"

Quinn sat back. "Ready," he said. "Let's go home."

COMING NEXT MONTH

#561 HE'S A REBEL by Linda Randall Wisdom
STUDS #3
Ukiah Jones thought he'd spend the week before Christmas holed up in his Tahoe cabin, alone and secluded. But the cabin was occupied—by ex-spy turned mother Sydney Taylor and her two little charges—who made Ki play Santa and daddy!

#562 THE BABY & THE BODYGUARD by Jule McBride
When Anton Santa was hired to protect the three-year-old mascot of a family toy store, he didn't realize the pint-size client was the daughter of his ex-lover, Cynthia Sweet. Santa meant to keep his identity hidden and research the truth: Had he accidentally been hired to protect his own daughter?

#563 THE GIFT-WRAPPED GROOM by M.J. Rodgers
Noel Winsome was absolutely determined that her pre-Christmas marriage to a Russian mail-order groom would be in name only. But when Nicholas Baranov held her under the mistletoe, Noel wondered how long she could wait to unwrap her presents....

#564 A TIMELESS CHRISTMAS by Patricia Chandler
When he appeared in her courtroom out of nowhere, Miguel de Pima reminded Judge Dallas McAllister of a long-lost lover...one who'd been hanged on Christmas Eve a hundred years ago. This Christmas they had to find a way to reunite a town divided by hate, or risk losing each other...again.

AVAILABLE THIS MONTH:

#557 ONCE UPON A HONEYMOON
Julie Kistler

#558 QUINN'S WAY
Rebecca Flanders

#559 SECRET AGENT DAD
Leandra Logan

#560 FROM DRIFTER TO DADDY
Mollie Molay

This holiday, join four hunky heroes under
the mistletoe for

Christmas Kisses

Cuddle under a fluffy quilt, with a cup of hot chocolate and these
romances sure to warm you up:

#561 HE'S A REBEL (also a Studs title)
Linda Randall Wisdom

#562 THE BABY AND THE BODYGUARD
Jule McBride

#563 THE GIFT-WRAPPED GROOM
M.J. Rodgers

#564 A TIMELESS CHRISTMAS
Pat Chandler

Celebrate the season with all four holiday books sealed with a
Christmas kiss—coming to you in December, only from
Harlequin American Romance!

AMERICAN ☩ ROMANCE®

Four sexy hunks who vowed they'd never take "the vow" of marriage...

What happens to this Bachelor Club when, one by one, they find the right bachelorette?

Meet four of the most perfect men:

Steve: **THE MARRYING TYPE**
Judith Arnold
(October)

Tripp: **ONCE UPON A HONEYMOON**
Julie Kistler
(November)

Ukiah: **HE'S A REBEL**
Linda Randall Wisdom
(December)

Deke: **THE WORLD'S LAST BACHELOR**
Pamela Browning
(January)

"HOORAY FOR HOLLYWOOD" SWEEPSTAKES

HERE'S HOW THE SWEEPSTAKES WORKS

OFFICIAL RULES — NO PURCHASE NECESSARY

To enter, complete an Official Entry Form or hand print on a 3" x 5" card the words "HOORAY FOR HOLLYWOOD", your name and address and mail your entry in the pre-addressed envelope (if provided) or to: "Hooray for Hollywood" Sweepstakes, P.O. Box 9076, Buffalo, NY 14269-9076 or "Hooray for Hollywood" Sweepstakes, P.O. Box 637, Fort Erie, Ontario L2A 5X3. Entries must be sent via First Class Mail and be received no later than 12/31/94. No liability is assumed for lost, late or misdirected mail.

Winners will be selected in random drawings to be conducted no later than January 31, 1995 from all eligible entries received.

Grand Prize: A 7-day/6-night trip for 2 to Los Angeles, CA including round trip air transportation from commercial airport nearest winner's residence, accommodations at the Regent Beverly Wilshire Hotel, free rental car, and $1,000 spending money. (Approximate prize value which will vary dependent upon winner's residence: $5,400.00 U.S.); 500 Second Prizes: A pair of "Hollywood Star" sunglasses (prize value: $9.95 U.S. each). Winner selection is under the supervision of D.L. Blair, Inc., an independent judging organization, whose decisions are final. Grand Prize travelers must sign and return a release of liability prior to traveling. Trip must be taken by 2/1/96 and is subject to airline schedules and accommodations availability.

Sweepstakes offer is open to residents of the U.S. (except Puerto Rico) and Canada who are 18 years of age or older, except employees and immediate family members of Harlequin Enterprises, Ltd., its affiliates, subsidiaries, and all agencies, entities or persons connected with the use, marketing or conduct of this sweepstakes. All federal, state, provincial, municipal and local laws apply. Offer void wherever prohibited by law. Taxes and/or duties are the sole responsibility of the winners. Any litigation within the province of Quebec respecting the conduct and awarding of prizes may be submitted to the Regie des loteries et courses du Quebec. All prizes will be awarded; winners will be notified by mail. No substitution of prizes are permitted. Odds of winning are dependent upon the number of eligible entries received.

Potential grand prize winner must sign and return an Affidavit of Eligibility within 30 days of notification. In the event of non-compliance within this time period, prize may be awarded to an alternate winner. Prize notification returned as undeliverable may result in the awarding of prize to an alternate winner. By acceptance of their prize, winners consent to use of their names, photographs, or likenesses for purpose of advertising, trade and promotion on behalf of Harlequin Enterprises, Ltd., without further compensation unless prohibited by law. A Canadian winner must correctly answer an arithmetical skill-testing question in order to be awarded the prize.

For a list of winners (available after 2/28/95), send a separate stamped, self-addressed envelope to: Hooray for Hollywood Sweepstakes 3252 Winners, P.O. Box 4200, Blair, NE 68009.

CBSRLS

OFFICIAL ENTRY COUPON

"Hooray for Hollywood"
SWEEPSTAKES!

Yes, I'd love to win the Grand Prize — a vacation in Hollywood — or one of 500 pairs of "sunglasses of the stars"! Please enter me in the sweepstakes!

This entry must be received by December 31, 1994.
Winners will be notified by January 31, 1995.

Name _____

Address _____ Apt. _____

City _____

State/Prov. _____ Zip/Postal Code _____

Daytime phone number _____
(area code)

Account # _____

Return entries with invoice in envelope provided. Each book in this shipment has two entry coupons — and the more coupons you enter, the better your chances of winning!

DIRCBS

OFFICIAL ENTRY COUPON

"Hooray for Hollywood"
SWEEPSTAKES!

Yes, I'd love to win the Grand Prize — a vacation in Hollywood — or one of 500 pairs of "sunglasses of the stars"! Please enter me in the sweepstakes!

This entry must be received by December 31, 1994.
Winners will be notified by January 31, 1995.

Name _____

Address _____ Apt. _____

City _____

State/Prov. _____ Zip/Postal Code _____

Daytime phone number _____
(area code)

Account # _____

Return entries with invoice in envelope provided. Each book in this shipment has two entry coupons — and the more coupons you enter, the better your chances of winning!

DIRCBS